THE HILL

Works by David Poyer

The Hemlock County Novels

Thunder on the Mountain * *As the Wolf Loves Winter*
Winter in the Heart * *The Dead of Winter* * *The Hill*

Tales of the Modern Navy

The Academy * *Arctic Sea* * *Violent Peace* * *Overthrow*
Deep War * *Hunter Killer* * *Onslaught* * *Tipping Point*
The Cruiser * *The Towers* * *The Crisis* * *The Weapon*
Korea Strait * *The Threat* * *The Command* * *Black Storm*
China Sea * *Tomahawk* * *The Gulf* * *The Passage*
The Med * *The Circle*

The Tiller Galloway Novels

Down to a Sunless Sea * *Louisiana Blue*
Bahamas Blue * *Hatteras Blue*

The Civil War at Sea

Fire on the Waters * *A Country of Our Own*
That Anvil of Our Souls

Other Books and Plays

Writing in the Age of AI * *F-35 (with Tom Burbage et al.)*
The Whiteness of the Whale * *Heroes of Annapolis*
Happier Than This Day And Time * *Ghosting*
On War and Politics (with Arnold Punaro)
The Only Thing to Fear * *The Shiloh Project* * *White Continent*
Star Seed * *Shadowland* * *Blood Moon* * *Waterwoman*

THE HILL

a novel

David Poyer

NORTHAMPTON HOUSE PRESS

Jacket art and cover design by NHP LLC.
ISBN (print edition) 978-1-950668-26-7
Library of Congress Control Number: 2023919955
Published by Northampton House Press, www.northampton-
house.com. Franktown Virginia USA.
Printed in the United States of America.

ONE

A hot and humid day in early October. The gleaming hardwood floor of the gym gave off a varnishy, polished smell as distinct from the miasma of sweaty bodies as a fife breaking into a piano concerto.

Phil Pirella reflected on that as he limped across the expanse of scuffed flooring, catching from the knot of scuffling and shouting basketball players at the far end another smell, an indoor kind of smell. The grandstands and the crowds at night and harsh lighting were in it too. Only the sweat was the same.

He was so concentrated on this usually neglected sense that a moment later he caught another whole family of mingled odors. The cheerleaders were standing in relaxed poses around Sheila Conrad, listening as she described the next routine. Some glanced his way as he walked by. Catching their looks, he turned his body away a bit, hiding the withered arm.

The girls looked back at Sheila as soon as they recognized him. No one else in the gym seemed to remark the thin figure, lurching under an armload of books, left arm curled tightly to its chest.

A stairwell led down to the track locker room. As he left the reverberating gleam of the gym behind, he caught from below the familiar cross-country smells; wintergreen oil, sharp and fresh, Grip-Tite and sweet rosin and peppery liniments and rubs. Soap and wet concrete, and of course the dank rubbery stink of old perspiration. The odors were linked, somewhere in the depths of his brain, to violent exertion, and his gut cramped, already preparing for the day's workout.

He bumped the heavy door open with his left shoulder, an action that looked natural enough with his right arm full of books. Stacking them on a bench, he spun the dial on his locker, threw them inside one by one, then started to undress.

Four o'clock, time for workouts to start, but only three other runners were dressing out, and there were twenty on the team. *Still early in the season,* he thought, *but Coach should put more pressure on the others to get out and run. We won't have much of a team otherwise.*

He didn't know all the guys yet, but he knew the three there now. Steve Rapisjek, a squat, dark, and silent reject from the jayvee football team, sat in one corner, lacing his shoes. Ray Bienvenito, apparently already finished for the day, was whistling dolefully in the shower, enjoying the dramatic echoes. Ray had fifth period free and ran while his teammates were in trig or social studies. And Carl Saarlo, the best quarter-miler the school boasted (though still only a junior) was pulling on his sweats across from Phil. He flashed a welcoming grin before his face disappeared under the Raymondsville High Tigers hoodie.

After a great working of arms his face, still grinning, emerged. He sauntered over to Phil's locker. Who meanwhile had gotten his supporter and shorts on without too much trouble. "How we doing today, buds?"

"Not too bad until fifth period." Phil wrestled his shirt on, the red-and-gold Raymondsville singlet normally worn only at meets, handling the left arm with his right to maneuver it in. "Reimer popped a surprise quiz on us, mostly about the last two experiments."

Saarlo laughed and started doing jumping jacks. "Hey, if I

2

had your average, I wouldn't be sweating one quiz."

Saarlo was a top runner, but he never looked down on the slower guys because of that. He was one of the few who treated Phil like a teammate and not like some kind of freak. He'd been the same way last year, during their first track season.

Phil held out his sweat pants. "Mind helping me?"

"Sure." The other junior held the waistband open at bench level as Phil leaned far back and stiffly maneuvered his left and then right legs into them. He gave Phil an arm up off the bench so he could finish pulling the pants up.

"Say, lemme ask you something. You're not the smartest guy I know – Kirkpatrick 'd take the medal for that – but I never see you without an armload of books, except when you're running, I mean. You trying to be another Einstein?"

Phil laughed. "Yeah, I spend a lot of time studying. And you're right, I'm no brain. But . . . I want to be a doctor."

"A doctor. Your old man's a cop, ain't he?"

"Yeah."

"I don't know shit about med school, Phil, but I know it takes a lot of money."

"Or else real good grades. I talked to Mr. Kroezler, the guidance counselor. And you can borrow from the government, and pay it back when you graduate. Anyway, that's why so much studying."

"You'll make it, buds." Saarlo punched Phil playfully on the right shoulder. "See ya on the track." And jogged out.

Phil took several more minutes to talcum his socks and inside his shorts and lace the light canvas shoes he wore for workouts. Across the room Rapisjek finished his own preparations, closed his locker, and looked around slowly. Noticing Phil for the first time, he nodded stolidly, without changing expression, and left too.

Phil pulled a sweatband on over his long dark hair. He'd

learned the value of thorough preparation during track season, as a sophomore. He hadn't done that great, hadn't lettered, and to be completely honest, hadn't been good enough to run in any of the meets. *But I learned a lot,* he thought. *And the exercise helps.*

Ready, he banged the locker shut, spun the combination lock, then jogged stiffly up the steps and outside, into the sunlight.

The old-fashioned cinder track crunched under his shoes. Emerging from the cool shade, he jogged stiffly across to the grassy oval in the center. Saarlo waved from the far corner of the quarter-mile-long track; the junior was doing a slow jog. Phil waved back and began his own warmup.

Running was hard, painful, and slow unless he prepared properly. With advice from Dr. Burnett and from Coach Anderson, he'd evolved a routine to stretch and warm each muscle, tendon, and ligament. It took longer than the other runners, but he never grudged the time. He thought of his body as a cranky machine, requiring long and usually painful maintenance.

He started with fifty jumping jacks, doing the exercise rapidly, on tiptoe to stretch his calves. With the last he went directly into a set of trunk-twisters, limbering up shoulders and midriff. He dropped and did five one-armed pushups, rolled to a sitting position, and followed them with fifty situps. The last ten were hard and he finished them puffing.

A light sweat broke and his heart was speeding up. He shook his legs out, then jogged a very slow half-mile, two laps around the track, concentrating on a smooth, relaxed stride.

As he rounded the second lap his eye was drawn by a flash of red hair at a window overlooking the track. Forcing his gaze back to the cinders underfoot, he ran on; but he did an extra lap, and looked again as he rounded the third lap. But there was no one at the window.

4

Back on the grass, he did an exercise normally used by hurdlers to stretch the tendons of the thighs and crotch. Next he did high kicks, stretching both legs to their limits, then concentrated his exercises on the weaker left leg. He ran two more quarter-miles, a little faster each time, starting each 440 from a crouch at an imaginary starting gun.

Now the blood was flowing. His bad left leg felt better, stronger; it no longer trailed in a limp. He kept alternating stretches and jogs. Finally, still jogging slowly, he looked down at the left arm, curled grotesquely against his chest, and tried to wiggle the limp fingers. Not bad, he thought wryly. *Another ten years of physical therapy and I might be able to scratch my balls.*

But he was warmed up now and it was time for some real running. Rapisjek was sitting on the bleachers, slowly rubbing his calves. Phil jogged over and asked him to keep time for a couple of 880-yard runs.

* * *

Mary Pirella opened the screen door and looked anxiously up the street for the ninth time since five o'clock. *Where can he be*, she thought, *It'll be dark soon. And it'll be too cold for him. He'll be coming home in a sweat again.* She shook her head wearily and went back to the kitchen, where she was preparing the mushroom sauce that Jacob, Phil's stepfather, liked with his spaghetti.

Mary Pirella was thin and worn-looking, a little sad-looking, though she'd been attractive once. Phil, her only child, was from her first marriage, a short one.

Although she and Jacob had wanted children they'd never come. For this, as for so many other things, she blamed herself.

Why won't he ever wear that warm jacket Jake got him for his last birthday? All he ever likes is that thin track jacket. She stirred the steaming sauce. *And that's nothing but nylon, it won't keep him warm.*

5

The screen door banged and she heard Phil's limping step going up the stairs to his bedroom. Then the squeak of his bed as he collapsed into it.

She squeezed her eyes shut over the simmering food to stop her tears. *Philip's lying up there exhausted again from that -- damned --* running, she thought. *He won't listen. He never admits to himself he just can't do all the things the other boys do.*

But with this thought her own guilt overwhelmed her. *It's not his fault, it's mine, mine. The doctors can call it what they want. But I was the one that was carrying him, after I left Bill. It was my drinking that did it. Before my baby was even born.*

Thank God she'd met Jacob after all the cruelty and ruin of her first marriage. He was the right man for her, steady and understanding. They'd never be rich, but policemen never got laid off, and there'd be a pension someday. She had so much to be thankful for.

But that didn't make her son well again. The Bible was right about the sins of the fathers. And mothers. Her abandon and drunkenness meant her son would go through life as a cripple. The priest said she was forgiven. But she could never forgive herself.

Jake got home. He went into the bedroom to change out of his uniform. She liked his broad shoulders and the manly way he carried himself. "Spaghetti tonight," she called.

"Good," came from the bedroom.

She went to the foot of the stairs. "Phil-lip! Time for supper."

"Not hungry, Mom."

"Philip, now come down here. You can't run and not eat. You'll get sick . . . Jake, make him come to dinner."

He limped downstairs at last. Not hungry? She noted his two big helpings of pasta, plus salad, dessert, and oatmeal cookies too, before he went back upstairs to start on his homework.

She took dessert into the living room and sat with her husband while he watched Joe Friday on television. She laughed at his sarcastic comments on TV crimefighting, and the night slipped gradually away, and for a time there she was content for the rest of the evening with him.

* * *

Cheshire Marzeau knew she was too tall, too lean, too angular to be beautiful. So she'd ordered her life accordingly. And to most of her students she was only a bony, awkward young woman whose earnest manner generally elicited the amusement of her English classes

This was her first year of teaching. Sometimes she wondered if her eagerness to fire a spark of enthusiasm in her pupils was just inexperience. That as her years accumulated her hopes would be reduced by innumerable gray days to ashes. But so far, she still hoped to find a few students who cared as much as she did.

Tonight she sat alone at her desk in her small, neat apartment, admiring the moonlight flooding the mapleshrouded drive outside her window and pondering how to arouse interest in the nineteenth-century English novel.

She was writing her lesson plan for the upcoming week. The standard approach to new material, which she'd carefully applied for the past month, was to arouse enthusiasm by a calculated combination of attention-getting, talking the new material up in advance, and pointing up the personal advantage to students of a knowledge of the subject. *Unfortunately,* she thought, *this might work for Mr. McGowan, the auto shop teacher.* His subject was elective, concrete, and the advantages were easily visualized: a steady job or a faster Ford. English, though, was loathed by most of the class as a grind. And she couldn't think of any personal advantage to an eighteen-year-old of a detailed analysis of Joseph Conrad's *Lord Jim*.

Yes, before her in the circle of yellow light from her desk lamp was the previous teacher's lesson plan. Written in black ink with a fine nib, the yellowed pages were cast in an unfamiliar format. After some study she could follow it, but how old Mrs. Gurlock had been able to read this was a mystery. Or maybe she'd just taught it for so many years she knew it by heart. Nor did it appear to have the first element of any lesson plan she'd seen in college. It had no student motivation at all. If Rebekah Gurlock had really followed this plan, she'd plunged directly into Conrad after "Seating the Class."

Seating the class? She suddenly realized the pages she was reading were older than she was. How did they expect her to follow this? She had neither the absolute authority over the students teachers had wielded forty years ago, nor the grasp of adolescent psychology decades of experience must make second nature. All she had, really, was a desire to teach a subject she loved, and a rote grasp of basic classroom principles.

Okay then . . . how could a critical reading of an outdated work of fiction benefit a teenager to whom the most carefully wrought prose could bring nothing more than confused and chaotic images culled from television or movies? The only terms in which she could reach them were those of their own world. What could Jim do for them?

And then she had it, and the moonlight outside, the silence of her bare apartment, and her loneliness were forgotten. Her long, spidery fingers flew over the keys as she recorded her own personal solution to the Why of Jim's cowardice, reinvention, and redemption.

Despite it, she didn't fail to include a reminder the novel would figure prominently in the mid-terms.

TWO

He fought, kicking hard with his good leg, but the nurses held him down. He was too young to understand, too small to do anything but scream with terror. The bright lights hurt his eyes. A masked woman put a cup over his mouth, and turpentine fumes whirled him down a spiraling tunnel. A black hole drew closer and closer until he fell through it into nothingness.

The alarm sounded by his bed and Phil opened his eyes. He was still shaking and breathing hard. The dream was so vivid it took him several minutes to convince himself he was eighteen, not five, and awakening from a nightmare and not from anesthesia.

He sat up in bed and rubbed his face, looking around at his familiar room.

A rack on the wall held four objects: a Winchester .22 lever-action Jake had given him when he was ten; a dark hardwood cane, rubber-tipped, dented with hard use and marked by a dog's teeth; a small yellow wood crutch, also battered and· chewed; and, at the top of the figured walnut rack, the steel axle of a child's wheelchair.

The dream was still strong in his mind, and the past sucked him back.

The first memories he could retrieve were of beds, doctors, and pain.

At Strong Memorial in Rochester the doctors had said they

could release the contractures, perhaps straighten the twisted leg, but there was little chance of the boy's ever walking without support. It was his stepdad who'd insisted on the operations, then on the long, excruciatingly painful months of therapy.

Phil shuddered as he recalled the third operation, when he'd been seven. The surgeon, a shy balding man, would bring hand-puppets on his rounds and pretend they were biting the children's withered arms and legs and chests. He'd spent hours carefully slicing the muscles, releasing and letting them lengthen again from where they'd tensed and contracted in to uselessness, replacing ligaments here and there with snippets from the hopeless left arm.

He raised his left leg and flexed the foot up and down. It had taken a year on the machines to learn that one motion.

He'd been sitting in his wheelchair at Strong, trying vainly to move his foot from time to time, as he had for months. Sitting there in the ward with the other kids around him, not paying much attention to the leg, and decided to roll around a little and see anyone wanted to play Chinese checkers, when his foot jerked. He'd been so excited he'd tipped the chair over and knocked himself cold against a radiator.

For a month after he'd gone crazy trying to move it again. But each time it happened the pathways became more accessible. A last operation had corrected the remaining deformation and made it possible to walk with a brace and a cane. But the muscles in the upper thigh were still too weak to move the leg forward in a normal manner. He'd had to swing his tormented, still-twisted leg with the left hip.

The alarm buzzed again and he snapped it off. Scissoring his right leg under his left, he lifted both and swung them out of the bedclothes to the floor. Everything was still stiff and weak in the mornings, but he was a hell of a lot better off than some of the others he'd known in the wards. *I ought to write to Donny and Jane more often*, he thought. They were still at Strong, unable to even breathe without the machines.

He dressed himself and went downstairs to the kitchen. The clock over the range said it was six-thirty. Mary and Jake were still asleep. He scrambled some eggs and ate them with toast and orange juice. He peered outside; a few clouds glowed in the sunrise. A nice day, he thought. I'll walk to school today. And, since the dream had made the past so vivid, he smiled. Yes, I'll walk.

* * *

As the third-period bell rang Alicia Ryan walked into Miss Marzeau's classroom. Without moving in their seats, the boys gave the impression of turning toward her as sunflowers follow the sun. The girls reacted in different ways. The more attractive sent dark glances her way. Those who were plainer or more studious had always found Alex gracious and friendly.

As she took her seat a shimmering mane of bright auburn hair settled softly about her shoulders. Those who'd known her in grade school swore it had always been that way; it had   never darkened, as most light hair will after childhood. She was of average height, but somehow seemed tall to the taller boys, and of just the right height to the average, and petite to the shorter. Her manner changed too, in the way best suited to win the admiration of her listener. She lived on admiration, and without a steady dose (as of some agreeable but treacherous drug) supplied by a circle of admirers of both sexes, she felt empty and bored. She tossed her hair back with a shake of her head and passed her hand over it with a delicate gesture.

To Sheila Conrad, a slight brunette who captained the cheer team, the cascade of russet hair was a red flag. To Myrna Hastings, who wrote sensitive poetry and dreamed of a boy who'd see beyond skin-deep lack of beauty, Alex was Grace and Beauty personified. To Fred Barnes, whom she'd dropped the day he was demoted to the second string, she was a hard and faithless woman who cared more for popularity than people. And to Phil, who sat behind her, she was the occasion of every sin of concupiscence his fevered brain could conceive.

Since his first sight of her he'd been seized by a desire so strong his previous infatuations seemed pure and platonic by contrast. It was pure and sacred lust. They shared two classes, Modern Living and English. The instructors in both courses had noticed his air of other-worldly abstraction, as if overmastered by some far-off goal; and although his homework and test grades were good, though not outstanding, they never knew, when they called on him, whether they were going to get anything pertinent in response.

In fact, he was fantasizing about Alex, even when he wasn't stealing glances. And his reveries of her were neither chaste nor impersonal.

Miss Marzeau stalked in with her quick stride and launched gamely into a buildup of some new book or other. Annoyed by her zealous manner, Phil thought, *Why is she trying so hard to sell us on this thing? It's just another old book.* He'd read it, maybe see what Myrna had to say about it, but he didn't feel like listening to Marzeau too. Particularly when She was sitting just ahead of him, smiling at the teacher, tossing that red, red hair, breasts bobbing as she moved.

He propped his head against his right arm and the teacher's voice faded to a dull ache. The less important stimuli ceased to reach his mind and a much more absorbing drama began to unfold, with himself in a title role.

They were kissing in the front seat of his Mustang. Alex and he had spent the evening drinking and dancing at the Hive, but he still felt cool-headed and intent, while she was hot and cuddly.

12

He'd parked off the main road, across a disused railroad spur, and they were screened from the road by heavy brush and the elevation of the embankment.

When he kissed her she moaned. Moonlight yellowed her hair and he stroked her neck. Her nipple was warm and hard, the way he'd read it should be in Jake's men's magazines. She responded with little shudders and moans.

The bucket seats changed to a bed and she was naked except for a filmy nightgown. He ran hishand down the length of her underneath it. Her flesh was hot and smooth. When she parted her legs for him it was warm there and hairless like the women in *Playboy*. Their eyes met in the near-darkness and she smiled at him, a loving, accepting smile.

She raised her hand to answer a question and suddenly he was back in the classroom, recalled by her motion. Somewhere in the more remote corners of the universe Marzeau was droning on about ships and lifeboats, interrupted now and then by a question, but directed at the other students, not at him.

Alex flashed him a conspiratorial smile and shifted on her seat, pulling her tweed skirt slowly down over her hips. She peeled off her tight red sweater and began unbuttoning her blouse, lingering over each button, teasing him. The rest of the class, oblivious of what she was doing, stared dully ahead at the chalkboard.

She had only her panties left, and was daring him to reach across the aisle for her, when the bell rang.

* * *

At five that afternoon he was into his fifth three-quarter-effort lap of the quarter-mile track when Coach Anderson, who'd been standing by the bleachers watching, waved him over. Phil slowed and trotted up.

13

"Pirella, let's talk about your workouts." Anderson took off his coach's cap and rubbed a graying, crew-cut scalp. "This's your first cross-country season, right?"

Phil jogged in place. In front of this muscular, fit man he was suddenly conscious of the useless arm curled against his chest. "Yessir, Coach. I ran track one season, sophomore year."

"Did you letter?"

"No, sir."

"What event?"

"Middle distance."

"Half-mile's not very far. Why didn't you go for two?"

"All the cross-country runners wanted to run the two-mile. I couldn't keep up. But I tried out for it."

"I'm sure you did." Anderson's gaze wasn't on Phil; he was following another runner around the track. "I normally don't heap compliments on my runners, especially this early in the season. I'm sure you know that?"

"I've heard it, sir," Phil said. He felt silly jogging in place and talking so he stopped.

"No, go ahead, stay loose." The coach took his dead, chewed cigar from his mouth and looked at it thoughtfully. "I don't want to interrupt your workout. But I wanted to say two things: first, that I do know about your – handicap – and I think just your being out here, trying, means you have more balls than a lot of the champs I've known. And second, if you continue to practice as hard as I've seen you work the last two weeks, you might get that letter this year."

"I'd really like that, Mr. Anderson."

"I know. And, one other thing. You're working out wrong."

"I am?"

"Oh, it's good enough for the 880, or even for the mile. And for some it might be okay to do ten good laps around a level track for cross-country, too. But I'll give you some advice; you

14

don't have to take it. D'you know Joe Brentano?"

"I know who he is. I've seen him around. But I don't know him well, sir."

"Brentano's probably the best cross-country runner in this part of the state. Last year we sent him to the AAU, State championships, and he took a fourth, All-State. He's a natural runner, and he has a kind of fire inside a coach doesn't see very often. It's like he has to win, or die. He has a personal workout he developed on his own. If you want, talk to him tomorrow, and maybe you can start running his course instead of working out on a track."

"Coach, if you think it'll make me a better runner, I'll do it," said Phil.

"Great." Anderson slapped him on the back. "I've held you up long enough. Now get outthere and finish your workout."

As Pirella jogged away, bobbing slightly each time his left leg moved forward, Anderson smiled grimly, his tanned, wrinkled face barely moving. The kid could never run in competition. The other coaches would laugh him out of the league. But he'd get his letter. He'd see to that if he had to face down the whole School Board.

* * *

The beat was quiet tonight, Jake Pirella thought. Lounging in his easy chair, feet up, nursing a can of Straub's, waiting for dinner. A small town didn't have much to compare to *LAPD* or *The Rookies*. After fifteen years of police work, first in Olean, another small town near the Pennsylvania Line, then for the last ten in Raymondsville, he could count on two fingers the number of times he'd drawn his .38. He'd never fired it off the range.

The lack of excitement was probably just as well for a family man. And the really important jobs were always mundane:

directing traffic near the Allegheny Plywood plant when work let out; checking the doors to the Main Street shops after the owners went home; keeping kids from getting in trouble back of the railroad embankment on Saturday nights; escorting the manager of the First Raymondsville around on paydays.

He ran his hand over thinning hair and sighed. Seemed like one day you're strong young buck, twenty-two, with a little action behind you, fresh out of the Corps and ready for anything and anyone.

And the next day you're into the Fat Forties, balding, pudgy, stuck in the dead-end job of a small-town cop, married, a house, a stepkid almost grown; a real solid citizen. . . .

What a humdrum fate for the wild kid he'd been.

He leaned forward to change the channel. It wouldn't be so bad, if the dreams faded when youth did. But the dreams and ambitions, the plans and fire never wholly left a guy, no matter how many compromises he made.

"Mary," he called, "Phil upstairs?"

"Not home yet, "she called from the kitchen.

The first time he'd seen the kid, Mary had taken him home to her mother, who was taking care of the little boy while she waitressed. He couldn't walk, but somehow he got into everything in the house. They'd taken to each other as soon as Jake picked him up. He never cried or complained, though the pain from those withered limbs, trying to grow but twisted by shrunken hands of dead muscle, must have been bad. And the operations . . . again, he'd never whined, always kept trying to move, stand, walk.

He caught a movement from behind his chair, then felt a kiss on top of his head. Why did she always kiss him on his bald spot? "Dammit," he said, "Don't do that."

"Sorry. You used to like that."

"Well, I don't," he growled. "Not while I'm watching the

news."

She was silent and presently he heard an agitated clatter from the kitchen. Damn it, he'd gone and hurt her feelings again. He heaved out of the recliner, set his beer on a coaster on the coffee table and went into the kitchen. She was taking the turkey out of the oven.

He waited till she had it safely on the counter, then took her by the shoulders from behind. "Sorry," he said, and kissed her softly on the neck.

She said nothing, made no move to turn around.

"It wasn't that I was watching TV." She was standing stiffly in his arms, still facing the range. "Mary, you listening?"

"I'm listening," she said in a smothered voice. He realized she was close to crying.

"It was my bald spot. You kissed me on my bald spot. I'm . . . kinda sensitive about that."

She was silent for a moment and then he heard a glad little laugh-sob. She turned suddenly and came into his arms, holding her face up to be kissed, and he saw that she really had been crying.

Just then the screen door slammed. *Damn that kid*, he thought, *he doesn't go out in the evenings and he comes home early today?* "Let's save it for tonight," he murmured in her ear, and she blushed a little and smiled into his shoulder, and he loved her for that blush and that smile.

"Turkey tonight, Philip," she called gaily, and Phil wondered all through the meal what the secret was his parents kept exchanging glances about.

THREE

The next day, Wednesday, dawned with a threatening overcast but by midafternoon it had turned sunny and hot. From his seat by the window of the physics classroom Phil watched heat waves shimmer up from the gravel-topped roof of the vocational ed wing. It was an ideal day for a really grueling workout. The sky had become almost cloudless, and in spite of the air conditioning the heat was reaching into the classroom.

He tried to concentrate or the chalkboard, where Mr. Reimer was explaining the behavior of molecules heated in a closed container. Eventually the lesson ended and he threaded the corridors between cheerful students and harried-looking teachers, stopping at his locker to drop off some of his books.

"Hi, Phil, you running again today?"

Myrna Hastings swung her locker closed and turned to face him. Her short pale hair framed her sallow face in an appealing way, but her timid manner and the protective way she hugged her books to her chest made her look like a small, frightened bird. Her face, too, reminded him of a bird's.

"Hi, Myrn. Yeah, I am."

"Isn't it awfully hot out to be running around?"

"That's the best time. Makes you sweat."

"Ugh. You take that really seriously, don't you?"

He didn't answer, sorting quickly through his binders. He clanged his locker shut, nodded goodbye, and ran eagerly down the stair to the gym.

He was the first one in that afternoon (Corrigan was probably still out on the track). He'd struggled out of his school clothes and was almost dressed out when Rapisjek plodded silently in. Phil said "Hi" but got only a grunt back. *Do you ever have a good day?* Phil thought.

Shit! Should I wear sweats? Gonna be mighty hot out there. He decided it would be wiser not to skimp; if it got windy he had to keep his legs warm or they'd cramp up on him. As he tied the waistband Joe Brentano came in. He carried no books and was smoking a Camel from a pack he kept in his sock. He glanced around, then sauntered over. "Pirella?"

"Yeah."

"Anderson says you want to try the Hill today."

Phil kept his voice level, not responding to the derision in the other's tone. Brentano was touchy and had a name around school as a fighter. Best not to get on his bad side. "Yeah, Coach said it'd be a good workout."

Brentano laughed and went into the john. After a moment his voice echoed out. "Two thick pair of socks and a lot of talcum powder. We'll be on asphalt most of the way. You get shin splints?"

"Not, uh, usually."

Brentano was silent. Phil took off his shoes, shook a generous amount of Mennen into his socks, and pulled on another pair over the first. When he put the shoe back on, his feet were cushioned, all right, but the toes were bound so tightly he couldn't wiggle them. *Well, maybe they'll loosen up during the run,* he thought.

"Be out on the track warming up, Joe," he called. Brentano didn't answer. Phil waited a moment, shrugged, then jogged clumsily out into the glare.

By the time Brentano finally came out Phil had gotten his

legs loosened up and was doing a slow jog around the track, concentrating on the rhythm of breathing and pace. Brentano stayed on the grass near the door and began to do stretching exercises. He looked incredibly lithe and flexible. After a few minutes of this Brentano jumped to his feet and motioned him over with a jerk of his head. Phil jogged over to join him on the grass.

"I don't think I ever seen you run before," the senior said. "What's wrong with your knees?"

"It's called cerebral palsy. Nobody knows what causes it. It takes some warming up, but I can move pretty good now. If I didn't exercise it'd be a lot worse."

"Christ." The other's face had taken on an expression of disgust. "Anderson didn't say he wanted me to nurse a cripple over the Hill."

So there it was. Phil fought a surge of bitterness. "Don't do me any favors," he said, controlling his voice. "Just do your normal workout and I'll try to keep up. I don't need nursing from anybody, school hero or not. So just cut the crap and let's run."

Brentano quirked his eyebrows sardonically. "Such language from a nice Italian boy. Okay, crip, you asked for it. First leg's a mile and a half out route 158. I take it slow to warm up. Don't push it the first couple miles or you'll die on the upgrades. Ready?"

"Yeah," Phil said. "And if you call me 'crip' again I'll beat you to death with my crutch."

"Oh, Christ. Let's go, Jim Ryun." The senior started off, and after a moment Phil followed, matching his pace but staying a few yards behind.

At a slow run, or a fast jog, the two runners turned onto the street, ran in place on the sidewalk while waiting to cross, then moved on up a slight incline out of town. The sidewalks reflected heat into their faces. The glare was intense.

Brentano stayed on the narrow strip of grass between the curb and the sidewalk, avoiding the concrete surfaces as much as possible. Phil followed at a distance of five or ten paces as they moved over a low hill, passed the last of the close-set town houses, and turned a corner, entering a two-lane country highway. The sidewalk petered out and they ran on the firm gravel-and-clay shoulder. A car sparkled on the road far ahead, rushed toward them, and slowed slightly as the driver caught sight of the gray-clad figures. Then it was past in a roar and a flash of color and, a second after it was gone, a blast of wind and dust.

Phil began to feel the first wave of tiredness that comes when the body first realizes the effort that will be expected of it, and tries to dissuade the stubborn mind. He knew this feeling and knew also that if he kept on at the same pace it would soon pass.

He kept his eyes on Brentano for the most part, glancing down from time to time to forestall a misstep or fall. Brentano plodded steadily on at the same measured rate, running gracefully without his heels touching the earth, swinging along, looking totally relaxed. He didn't look as if he was expending an erg more than necessary to keep his body in motion.

The first resistance of Phil's body passed and he was running well. The dry heat from the sun, reflected from the clay and asphalt beneath his feet, seeped through the heavy cotton and melted into the sweaty heat of his muscles. A prickle broke across his scalp and he pulled an arm across his forehead in mid-stride. Ahead Brentano swerved onto the hard surface of the road as the shoulder contracted to a strip of mud, rising sharply to a bank covered with wild strawberry and goldenrod. He glanced back over his shoulder and Phil thought, *Yeah, the Crip's still back here.* He moved onto the asphalt and was jarred at each step by its totally unyielding surface. He came up off his heels, running with toes and calves, but still felt the shock in his legs and knees. It wasn't like running on cinders or grass.

Gradually the two runners entered a long, gentle decline, bordered on both sides by dark, sweet-smelling pine woods. Here and there the remains of old logging roads led off into the shadowy forest, the small trees growing between the grassy ruts testifying to their desuetude. Both boys were well into their running paces by now, each keying the rhythm of his footfalls to the longer rhythm of his breathing. Phil was consciously keeping to what he thought of as his distance running rhythm: a long breath in, beginning on the left foot, marked in the middle by the right, and continuing till the left fell again; a quick breath out, the exhalation taking one step, then a fraction of a second's rest for his lungs until the left foot came down again and the next inhalation began. Once he got into it, this rhythm fit his stride and didn't leave him gasping. It could be picked up a little by lengthening the stride and deepening each breath. He had two faster modes; for a sustained burst, he dropped the rest step and started each successive in-breath on alternate feet. And if the end of a race called for a sprint to the finish, he could take a breath on each stride.

They reached the end of the downgrade and Brentano pointed to the left with a finger, languidly, without affecting his deerlike lope. A moment later he turned into the pine-shadowed mouth of a single-lane macadam road.

The dark and coolness enveloped the fleeting figures like a rain shower. Phil gasped with delight. The air felt icy on his streaming face. A light wind chilled his wet sweat clothes. The sun, baffled by the intertwined branches above them, strobed through the foliage. Miniature sun-images danced on the shadowed road.

Brentano raised his arm and pulled his clenched fist sharply downward, twice, and they picked up the pace. The road began to climb and curved to the right. A gap in the trees allowed a glimpse of cattail-bordered ponds. A brown rabbit scuttled across the road ahead of them, panic-stricken, dodging this way and that.

As they rounded the curve the slope grew steeper. Phil leaned forward, digging at the road with his toes, and began to exert more effort to maintain speed.

Brentano, in the lead, remembered now he'd seen Pirella at track meets the year before, though the track coach had never put him in if anyone else was available, and sometimes even left a lane vacant rather than start him. Remembering that, he'd expected the junior to quickly fall behind, or feign some injury. Instead, through the two and a half miles so far, each time he'd looked back the kid had been sticking like glue. He ran with a hitch in the left leg, but kept up. Still, he thought, any freshman in decent shape could pull three miles on the level. The test lay ahead. One proved, or broke, the mind and heart of a would-be cross-country competitor.

The grade steepened still more, and began to curve back to the left. The boards rattled hollow as they pounded over a rickety plank-and-iron bridge spanning a limpid, rocky little stream.

A straight stretch of slight gradient opened ahead. They were pressing harder now, at a run, not a jog, and Phil's heart began to pound in his ears. His calves hurt from the constant upward grade and the effort of staying on his toes, and his shins began to pain from the unyielding hardness of the road. He wasn't getting enough air, so he shifted to the second rhythm. But all in all his wind was holding up. The sun was looming above them again, and in a moment his already damp shirt was dark with new moisture. The heavy trousers flapped and dragged at his legs. Now he wished he hadn't worn them.

The end of the straight stretch came into view ahead. It looked as if they were approaching the top. Brentano, a hundred feet ahead, reached the crest and disappeared from sight. Phil dug his toes into the pavement and strained to catch up. His calves and thighs hurt in earnest now.

He reached the top only to find that the road made a shallow turn and continued up at an even steeper grade than before. Brentano was almost out of sight around another bend.

With head lowered and arms pumping Phil forced his reluctant legs to move faster. His breathing seemed to give no relief from a terrible need for air. A leaden feeling began to invade his legs. His jaw clenched; he forced it to relax, then found his neck muscles tensed too. He bent still farther forward and strained his gaze upward, hoping for the crest, but found only sky overhead.

When he reached the top the road ran level for perhaps a hundred feet, then began a gently sinuous series of curves downward into a wooded valley. Here and there he looked down on the dull green and red roofs of a few scattered farmhouses.

His legs were so pleased with the downward course that he breezed cheerfully past Brentano, who'd slowed his pace and seemed to be flowing down the hill like a lanky, gray-clad stream. "Whoo!" the senior called, sounding amused. "Better take it easy on the downhill."

"The Hill," panted Phil, throttling back a little and trying to match the economy of Brentano's downhill roll, "wasn't," breathe, breathe, breathe, "too hard at all."

Brentano glanced at him, and a sardonic grin creased his sweaty face. Without a word, he pointed ahead.

Phil looked up, a mile or more across the pretty valley below, and saw the silver thread of road shining in the late afternoon sun, towering upward on the side of a massive mountain, steep, forbidding, threatening, utterly impossible.

He shut his eyes for an instant at his incredible stupidity, the rashness and naivete of his foolish boast. The Hill lay ahead, not behind, and his left thigh was weakening. Saying nothing, he throttled back and settled behind the lead runner, concentrating now on nursing his left leg.

They reached the valley bottom. The winding road was now two full lanes with a generous berm on either side. Orchards and plowed fields flanked it and the smells of warm earth and fertilizers reached them as they ran. They passed tin-roofed houses surrounded by rusting, useless car bodies. At one home they were noticed by a small yellow dog dozing in the sun. Their motions, the snap of their clothing, woke it, and it called joyously to every dog within hearing. Dashing out after them, it made furious rushes and prudent retreats until realizing it was being ignored; then it turned aggressive, and tried to bite Brentano's leg. He stopped short; the dog's momentum carried it past, and in one stride Joe caught up and kicked it hard in the belly. They left it kicking and barfing in the road, and ran on without looking back.

The level part of the road was all too short, and it soon began to rise once again. *If my leg hadn't started to give out,* Phil thought, *I might have gotten a little rest from that flat stretch.* As Brentano apparently had; he looked as fresh as when they'd started from the grounds half an hour ago. Instead, he'd had to put more of the load on his right leg, and now he felt as if he was almost hopping along. He was also getting a stitch in his side.

Brentano picked up the pace, not looking back as he did so.

They left the highway behind and ran on in the afternoon sun, now lower in the sky but still pouring out floods of heat and light. The road, now a single-lane blacktop with deep drainage ditches cut in the clayey soil on either side, side, climbed more steeply; its slope was just sufficient to hide the Hill rising behind it, though Phil could still sense its looming presence.

A decrepit tractor and harrow gradually overtook the runners, who moved to the narrow margin next to the ditch to let it pass. The aged farmer who drove it waved slowly to them. He knew little of running, but he knew the gaits of horses and children, and it was evident to his old eyes, squinched against the sun, that the second boy couldn't hold up much longer. There was something wrong the lad's hip . . . he wondered how far they were going, how far they'd come already, and whether the offer of a lift would be taken as an insult. But he remembered the pride of his own youth and kept silent. The tractor drew slowly away from them, the rusty harrow jouncing and blundering along behind.

Brentano hadn't been thinking about the other runner for a while. The steepening grade riveted his attention. His mind was absorbed in a continuous and critical monitoring of a flood of sensory input. He was like a pilot or a racing driver, so immersed in a machine that each tremor or unaccustomed sound was instantly caught and felt as pain or alarm.

The long level run and the small hill had taken the edge of readiness off his body and it was starting to hurt. He felt it at the bottom of his chest, in his mouth, parching from the hot, dry air, and in his thighs and calves. The sharpest and most insistent pain came from his shins, the muscles lining the front of the bone of the lower leg. Hundreds of miles on concrete, asphalt, hard-surfaced roads bad separated them from the bone and inflamed them. Now each step, cushioned though it was by extra layers of socks and extra-thick soles, sent a shaft of pain lancing up through his legs. The sun had given him a headache, and his weak eyes found it hard to focus on the shimmering pavement ahead.

His searching mind returned to itself with less of an evaluation than a resolution: he'd get over today. His legs could hurt all they wanted. That wouldn't make him go any slower or stop any sooner.

The grunting passage of the tractor drew his attention. The old coot driving the thing — what was that crazy gizmo he was dragging? — was looking back at the trailing runner, a puzzled expression in his shifty little eyes.

Brentano turned round and jogged uphill backward. The crip was keeping up, but now he was running like a crip. His stride was gone; his whole left side was lagging; he was trying to drag it along with spasmodic thrusts of the right leg. His head was down and his jaw was clenched. How long had he been running like this?

He jogged in place, watching, then circled him. The junior struggled forward, wrapped in his effort, and didn't even notice him. The interruption of the demanding rhythm he'd painfully set up left Brentano suddenly very tired. He came up on the other runner's left.

"Hey, gimp," he shouted, almost into his ear. Phil flinched but kept running.

"You can't hot dog it up the Hill like this."

"I'll make it," Phil gasped.

"Like hell, you will. I can't . . . slow down to . . . keep you company. I'm goin' on ahead."

"Okay."

Brentano pulled ahead, then turned back and matched Phil's pace again. "Come on . . . Phil," he said. "Stretch your stride out. Relax."

"Can't."

Sudden anger, fueled by his own pain, flared in Brentano's face. "You lousy quitter. I thought you had . . . some balls. Guess I . . . was wrong. You ain't a cripple . . . just a goddamn bagger."

Phil lunged at him, but the senior backpedaled easily from the weak blow, wildly thrown. He laughed pityingly, then turned and almost sprinted up the slope. Phil found himself rapidly outdistanced. Then the surge of adrenaline triggered by the mocking words spent itself. His left leg crumpled and he fell full-length on the hot asphalt. The other runner, almost out of sight over the upward swell of the Hill, didn't look back.

Phil felt tears burn and fought them back. He panted. The asphalt burnt his hands and face. After a few minutes he found the strength to roll off the road. The dirt of the bank felt cool and he lay there, one arm dangling over the edge of the ditch, until he could breathe, had suppressed the tears that made his eyes ache.

He got up slowly. Brentano, whom Phil realized he'd have to hate now, was nowhere in sight. His left leg felt flaccid and lifeless. His sweat clothes were wet and dirty, with spots of tar from the road and clay-and grass-stains from the berm. Limping badly, he trudged slowly up the Hill. The road circled partially around the rise to reduce the sharpness of the grade, but it was still so steep in places he had to place his feet sideways to walk without straining his calves. How did Brentano run this stretch? Did he zigzag back and forth across the road, or plant his feet sideways as he ran?

The height of the summit, when at last he reached it, was incredible. He turned and looked far out over the valley they'd left behind. The first small hill appeared from here to be only a slight rise, over which he could see almost all of Raymondsville. Haze dimmed the east of town. Long shadows from the surrounding hills stretched over vast tracts of field and forest.

A small sign at the very top gave the hill a proper name. Porcupine, elevation three thousand feet above sea level.

Phil decided his leg felt a bit better. After a short rest at the top, during which he forgot his misery for a little while in the beauty of the lengthening shadows, he jogged very slowly down the far side. It wasn't as steep as the approach, and he let the grade carry him gently down for about a mile. The sun was gone now and it was getting darker rapidly. The air was cool. He came to a crossroads and stopped. Which way back? Which way had Brentano turned?

Two bright headlights, set close together, approached from the left. Phil recognized the tractor that had passed them earlier. The same man rode it, now looking tired. Clods of dark earth fell from the swaying harrow. The farmer saw him and slowed.

"Need a ride, boy?" he called above the clatter of the engine.

"You headed toward Raymondsville?" asked Phil.

The farmer nodded and swung a thumb toward the rear of the tractor. Swallowing what little remained of his pride, Phil climbed up behind hm.

He was grateful to the old man for saying absolutely nothing to him for the rest of the long ride back.

FOUR

When he opened his eyes and tried to get up Phil winced in agony.

Every part of his body hurt except his left arm. *Maybe I should be grateful for that*, he thought, but he wasn't.

Washing his face, he noted with shame his eyes were red and swollen. *I can't go to school like this*, he thought. An aspirin would take care of the soreness, but red eyes – ?

After some thought, be soaked a washcloth in cold water, letting it run for a long time and thinking of the deep reservoir outside town from which it came. Jake had taken him fishing there once. He held the washcloth over his eyes till he convinced himself they looked normal.

He threw back two Bayers, finished dressing, and went downstairs to the kitchen.

It was still very early and the windows were dark. Should he run in to school? No, better save his energy. What if Anderson wanted him to try the Hill again that afternoon? That decision made, he began to quietly fix himself some breakfast.

Mary came in, in her nightgown, while he was frying sausage. "My, that smells good, Philip," she said. "Want me to make pancakes?"

"No thanks, Mom," he said quietly. He dropped bread in the toaster and got orange juice from the frosted pitcher in the fridge.

His mother sat at the table and watched him move busily about the kitchen. He could use only the one arm, but watching him, she thought he didn't really need another, his movements were so easy and natural.

"Philip, your eyes look red. Are you getting another cold?"

"Maybe."

"I wish you wouldn't run to school in the mornings, when it's so cold," she said. "I know you do it to try to keep up with the other boys on the team, but you can't if you're all tired out and have a cold from running in the morning."

"I'm not running this morning, Mom." The toaster popped and he snatched out the hot bread, holding it by the tips of his fingers.

"You have to think of your health."

He assembled sausage and toast on his plate, sat across from her, and started wolfing them down.

"My goodness, chew your food, Philip," his mother said. "You'll get a stomach-ache next."

She felt so frightened for him. What were they doing to him in that public school? He was growing so rough and mean. *I wish he wouldn't run, and study so hard,* she thought. *But whenever I try to make him stop he looks at me that way. Or gets mad and shouts at me. I wish Jake would talk to him. Maybe he could find out what's the matter. Maybe I should go and see his teachers. All this running, he's going to put himself back in a wheelchair.*

She felt the guilt eating steadily at her soul until she felt she couldn't go on. It wasn't his fault he couldn't do the things all the other boys could. It was hers. *If I hadn't drunk so much, he might be normal.* He was right to be short with her. She forgave him.

She reached across the table and patted his arm. Surprised and displeased, he scowled up at her. "I'm going back to bed," she said. "Have a good day at school."

He relaxed. "Sure, Mom."

31

When she left he looked at the clock over the stove. He stacked the dishes in the sink, picked up his books and homework papers from the dining-room table, and struggled into his track jacket.

At school it was seven-thirty and the corridors were thronged. As usual; but he had a strange sensation as he neared his locker. Were those curious glances from the people he passed? At the lockers, Steve Rapisjek was at his locker. "Hey, Steve," Phil said. The other runner looked past him, then walked away without a word or change of expression on his dull peasant's face.

Oh, Jesus, Phil thought. *That son of a bitch must have spread it all over the team I quit on him up on the Hill.*

Ray Corrigan walked by whistling. He saw Phil and faltered, then resumed, with a different tune. His gaze slid past.

"Oh, go to hell, both of you," said Phil, suddenly disgusted with the childishness of their actions. He walked away, leaving them both looking after him.

It was hard to concentrate that morning. He found himself listening for snickers and whispers when he got up to put a trig problem on the board. And of course, he blew it. Mrs. Brodie stopped him after class and warned him she expected more in the way of attention that he'd shown that day.

Myrna Hastings smiled at him in the hall but he was walking fast with his head down and didn't see her.

* * *

Alex Ryan had heard the story the night before. Now, at lunch, she was sitting with her small circle of admirers when Pirella came out of the lunch line with his tray and tried to find a place to sit. He approached table after table but the empty seats were "saved". At last he joined the commercial ed students at the far end of the cafeteria. They cheerfully shoved over and continued to talk animatedly among themselves, while he ate rapidly without speaking to them.

She'd heard it direct from Joe, but wondered what it sounded like now after being passed from mouth to ear through the school. She turned to Sheila Conrad."Sheila, honey, tell me - why the hex on Pirella? What's he done?"

"Oh, haven't you heard?" Sheila seemed surprised. "This Pirella – he's crippled, but he's got a big mouth – was bragging he could outrun everybody on the cross-country team, so Mr. Anderson, he's the coach, told him to race Joe Brentano."

"Brentano! Oh, he's dreamy!" said a small, plump freshman farther down the table. The older girls glared at her.

"Then what happened?" said Alex.

"He quit when he saw how hard it was, and when Joe tried to get him to try, Pirella tried to hit him."

The girls, who'd all been listening, gave vent to their indignation in various ways. Brentano was tall, good-looking, and a state champ. His parents owned a chain of local drugstores.

"That little runt."

"I'll bet Joe laughed when he swung at him."

"They won't let him run at meets. I saw him last year on the sidelines, limping along with that arm all curled up – yecch!"

"I heard he threatened Joe. His dad's a cop."

"He's always been like that. I knew him in third grade. He was on crutches then."

Only Alex was silent. Like a shrewd speculator in an uncertain market, she was too clever to join immediately in any crowd feeling. She remembered how Pirella was always checking her out in English. It had amused her, but it counted in his favor.

Sheila, laughing with the other girls, noticed her silence.

"Alex, don't you think that was a terrible way to behave to Joe?"

Alicia looked down at her tray and toyed with her fork a moment. She composed her lips into a judicial frown. "Sheila," she said slowly, "you know I don't condemn somebody just on the basis of some gossipy story."

The implied rebuke landed like a bombshell. The table fell silent. Sheila blushed. How she hated – yes, and feared – Ryan, always so cool and stuck-up and stealing every boy anyone had a date with. "It's no story," she said weakly into the silence. "It happened just yesterday, it really did."

"Well, we don't know what really happened, do we?" Alex asked sweetly. She paused, then added thoughtfully, "Actually, I think Phil's kind of cute. He's in my English class. And he's smart, too."

The others stared with mingled horror and admiration. Sheila saw instantly how she'd been outmaneuvered, and how Alex could now pose as the champion of the poor handicapped boy, while she got cast as the cold-hearted, gossipy bitch. Well, she'd play one more card before she conceded. "I wonder what Joe would think if he heard you saying that. Don't you have a date with him Friday?"

Alex turned to face her. "Look, Shelia," she said coolly, fully aware of the dozen girls hanging on her next lines, "I don't do things or say things behind people's backs. I don't care what Joe thinks. If he doesn't like it maybe he'll break the date and go out with you. I'm sure you'd love to break Joe and me up, wouldn't you?"

Sheila searched for words and found none. Pale with anger, she muttered, "Oh, you can kiss it, Ryan," seized her tray and left the table. She heard the others laughing as she left, and another low comment from Ryan, followed by a louder burst of laughter. *Bitch*, she thought redly. *For that, I will tell Joe. See how you like that.*

She didn't realize Alex had intended her to do that very thing.

* * *

Cheshire Marzeau noticed Phil's late entrance into third period, as did everyone else. He strode in without looking at anyone and slammed his books on his desk before throwing himself into his seat. He propped his chin on his hand and stared moodily ahead.

He was obviously upset and this bothered her a little. He was one of the two or three students she felt eager to see and teach each day. The others sat quietly enough, but they were inert, unimaginative, and cared mainly about their grades. Pirella, along with Linda Dunleavy and Myrna Hastings, sometimes came alive in class. Sometimes a light seemed to pop on behind his eyes, and he'd ask a question that showed real insight. Just too bad it happened so seldom. Most of the time his attention was far away, probably on one or another of the girls.

Today, though, he didn't look at her or raise his hand once. Troubles at home? She wished she could help. As the period drew to an end she gave out a quick reading assignment. The bell rang and they got up to leave.

"Phil," she said quickly, "May I see you at my desk for just a moment?"

He came over unwillingly and stood in front of her. She noted that his fist was clenched, knuckles white.

"Is something bothering you, Phil? You didn't seem to get much out of today's lesson."

To her relief he smiled. "A little," he said. "It'll pass."

She smiled back. "That's good. You're a good student. I wish there were more like you taking the advanced placement classes."

35

He looked down. What a cute boy, she thought, then surprised herself by reaching out and patting his hand, lightly, twice. "I'm sure things will look brighter tomorrow. Don't let it take your mind off *Lord Jim*. Conrad's going to have some important things to say to us a little later on."

"Okay, Miss Marzeau." He stood there a moment longer and when she nodded in dismissal he turned and left. He limped and she wondered if there were something wrong with his leg, too. That arm of his, such a pity. He really wasn't bad-looking.

* * *

To Phil's surprise Alex Ryan was waiting in the corridor. He was so taken aback he almost kept walking. Her smile was as radiant as her hair, and he noted with shock that he'd left a lovely, intimate fragrance out of his fantasies.

"Phil," she said.

"Uh, hi!"

She turned away but tipped her head for him to walk beside her. "Phil, you're pretty good in English, right?" She was still smiling up at him.

"Uh, I'm okay, I guess. I kind of like to read, I guess."

"You have French next, don't you?"

"Uh, no. Modern Living, with Hartlake. Same as you."

"Oh, of course!" She laughed. "I forgot. Sorry!"

"I sit toward the back. And it's kind of a big class. You might not have seen me."

At a turn in the corridor she stopped, standing close to him. He stopped too and looked down ather. Her perfume eddied up into his brain, then down to his loins.

They were standing there when Brentano came around the corner. His eyes grew wider, then his glance slid away and he walked past to his locker. Alicia smiled once more at Phil and said, "Well, we'd better start walking if we want to get there in time," and turned away

"Uh, so long, uh, Alex." He pulled himself together and stared after her erect figure. *Have to think this over*, he thought, but then he didn't think at all and just started after her like a bloodhound on a rare scent, forgetting the depression that had dogged him all day, and in truth, as he followed her down the crowded corridor, he could distinguish her scent from those of all the others.

* * *

There was no one in the locker room that afternoon to help him with his sweats, so when Anderson came in he was still struggling with them. "Pirella," the coach said. "You get a crack at the Hill yesterday?"

"Yes, sir. But I didn't make it all the way."

Anderson laughed. "I'd of been surprised if you did, on the first try. It took Joe the better part of his first season to work up to where he could take it in one go. I've been coaching here for seven years, and I can say if you can make it up Porcupine without a rest stop you've had a good workout."

"Yes, sir," Phil said.

"Imagine you're pretty sore today?"

"A little. Yeah." Actually he could barely move his left leg, but he didn't want to sound like a crybaby.

"If you'd given it your best, you'd be more than a little sore. Anyway, here's what I want you to do today. Do your own stretching routine for twice as long as usual. Then do ten half-effort laps on the track. Run a lap, walk a lap, run, total twenty laps. Got it?"

"Yessir," he said, relieved. "Stretch for double the time, then ten fifty percent laps, walk a lap between each one."

"That and a hot shower should relieve most of the soreness and tire you out. Actually I only want you to run the Hill twice a week. More often, that could tear you down more than it builds you up. Okay, get out there – hey, Saarlo! C'mere a minute."

He ran and walked his laps alone; he saw no reason to invite the contempt of the others. Some, like Carl Saarlo, he'd thought of as friends, but had they too been turned against him? At least Anderson didn't seem to have heard whatever was going around.

Toweling off after the shower, he was surprised at how good he felt. Both the soreness and the slight fatigue from today's laps were goth gone, leaving him loose, a little weak, but with a delicious warm sensation all over his skin. He decided to walk home rather than take the late bus.

* * *

She was showering with him. He held her close in the carpeted bathroom as she unbuttoned his shirt. Her blouse unbuttoned easily too. He unfastened her bra and she rubbed her nude breasts against his chest. Then she unbuckled his belt and ran her fingers along the length of him. They undressed quickly. Her hips framed a hairless triangle that drew his gaze like a magnet.

He shifted his books on his hip and waited for the light at First and Maple to change.

Under the million hot needles of the shower Alex moaned as he soaped her breasts. She clung to him and shuddered. "Oh, Phil," she murmured. "Oh, please do it to me, now, it's so lovely. . . . "

He was home before he knew it.

Mary had boiled chicken and heavy, doughy dumplings ready. Mike was home early for a change, sitting in front of the TV and reading *Sports Illustrated.* "Honey, Phil's home," he called. "How ya feelin', tiger?"

"Petty good. Coach gave me an easy workout today."

38

"You hungry, Phil?" called his mother from the kitchen.

"Sure am, Mom."

She came into the living room wiping her hands on her old blue and white apron. "Well, I guess everything's ready then. Jake, turn off that television."

* * *

It started to rain that night while he was doing his homework upstairs. He stopped around ten and sat at his desk looking out the little dormer window at a street light. The rain pattered steadily on the roof just above his head.

He was thinking about Alex Ryan again, but seriously this time, without daydreaming. Wondering whether he should ask her out.

But could he? He'd fantasized about her, but never seriously considered a date. Everyone knew she'd been going with Fred Barnes, but had dropped him for Brentano when Barnes had been dropped from the first string. Ergo, she liked winners, athletes, and guys with cars. Barnes had a Mustang, and Brentano drove that new blue convertible his dad had bought him.

Jake didn't make enough on the force to afford a car.

At that moment his gaze fell on the black-and-white cruiser parked in front of the house. The rain drew a silver haze around it in the light of the street lamp.

No, that would be ridiculous. It was Town property. It would get Jake in trouble, even if he let him, which he wouldn't.

He couldn't envision Alex on the town bus with him, so that left the taxi. He had a little cash left from his summer job cleaning the doughnut glazing machine and mopping up at Dopel's. A movie, then maybe a Coke at the Keynote downtown? Not very exciting for her, he thought.

She really is nice, he thought. Being so friendly today, when everybody else was so mean and childish. He felt ashamed of his fantasies about her. Who was he, anyway? Just a failure, a crippled nobody who never got to run in the meets, and she was only the most beautiful and popular girl in the whole school.

He turned out his study lamp and went down to the bathroom to brush his teeth. When he went to say goodnight both his parents were asleep in front of the late show. He went back upstairs, undressed, and got into bed. The sheets were cold.

What a day, he thought. *Pretty lousy at first. But if Alex really likes me I can take anything.* He saw her face again as she smiled up at him in the corridor. His hand found his crotch, then paused.

No, he resolved, *I will not do it again tonight. And I will not think any more dirty thoughts about such a good person.*

He fell asleep smiling.

FIVE

When he woke Friday morning it was the same as any other morning until he saw, outside his window, a square of dark, turbulent sky and recognized the patter of a fine rain. He reached out and reset his clock. He could take the school bus with a clear conscience. Then he remembered the day before, and knew he wouldn't be getting back to sleep.

He'd ask her out. Fine, that was resolved. But it brought up another problem; how? For some reason, the way he'd do it, the exact phrasing and tone, seemed important.

Lying in bed, he smiled. *If she wants to go out with me, she'll go. If she doesn't, she won't. I just have to have the words ready so that I don't just stand there with my mouth open the way I did when she spoke to me.*

At last hunger overcame his slothful desire for the warm bedclothes. He got up and dressed. It was still too early if he was taking the bus, but his stomach was growling. *Just a minute*, he thought, *be patient! You 'll be full soon.*

In the kitchen, he reviewed the availables and decided on toast. He had twelve pieces, with tea and orange juice, before he began to feel full. He cleaned up and lay down on the worn old living-room couch for a quick nap before the bus.

Standing in the rain at the bus stop he felt dry and warm under his raincoat. A pleasant feeling radiated from his stomach. Heightening his feeling of well-being was the anticipation of seeing her again. Some primary-graders were shouting, punching each other and stamping in the puddles, and he watched with an indulgent smile. The world, for a little while at least, was a beautiful place.

* * *

Cheshire had only a small breakfast, as usual. She wasn't hungry right after she got up. *But,* she thought, picking at a grapefruit half, *I make up for it at lunch, and then some.*

Wolfie pawed at her skirt, and she patted her lap. He jumped up and settled down in a ball, but his warm white cat self stayed tense, and his head moved to follow each spoonful. "Want some?" she asked. He indicated he did and she put a spoonful to his nose. The cat sniffed and made a face, turning his head away. He did this with such offended dignity, squeezing his eyes as if to say "How dare you offer this offal to me, Thomas Wolfe," that she laughed and hugged him and ruffled his fur. The cat took this in good humor, but jumped down from her lap and began prowling around the little apartment.

She finished breakfast and washed the bowl, placing it and the spoon in its proper place in the neat little kitchenette. She liked to wash dishes as she used them; then they didn't pile up and make a mess.

Before she left for class, she swept the little apartment with a critical glance. Not much furniture, but she disliked clutter. Everything was clean and in its place. And here came Wolfe, trotting up to say goodbye. "I love you, Wolfie," she whispered into his fur. She checked that his water bowl was full and locked the door behind her.

Her new car was parked in front. She stopped for a moment before getting in to admire it. Freshly waxed, its wet surface reflected her face. She settled into the seat and reached for the ignition. *It's been raining all night*, she thought, remembering the trouble she'd had with her old car. *I wonder if it'll start.* It did, with a powerful roar, at the first try. *Good car,* she thought. She loved it, too. And everyone said she drove it so well.

She raced the engine, then laughed out loud as she sent it lunging through the overwash of a creek, sending cascades of water to either side like a small red speedboat.

* * *

He'd decided to ask Alex at lunch. He'd thought about it a lot. He could ask in class, but that was too public. He could phone, but that was impersonal. No, it was best face to face, but now, standing in line with his tray, he felt as he did in the minutes before a race, waiting for the coach to decide whether to put him in or not. Though he never had . . . he loaded his tray up with something or other and limped slowly out into the crowded lunchroom.

Alex and Sheila and the rest of the girls were just sitting down when Cindy Robaley let out a squeak, hand to her mouth. Phil had come up to the table and was standing behind Alex with his tray in his right hand. They all turned at once, following Cindy's look, and stared at him.

"Hi, Alex," he said.

She turned to see who it was, and after a moment, smiled up. "Why, hello, Phil. What a surprise. Are you going to sit with us?"

The girls exchanged wide-eyed looks, but no one said anything.

He said, "Oh, no, thanks. Two or three of the . . . of the guys are holding a seat for me. I just, uh, wondered if you'd like to see a movie with me tomorrow night."

"Why, Phil," Alex began, and looked around the circle of expectant faces. Waiting, probably, for the mortal thrust of humiliation she'd deal him. Instead she turned back to him and smiled."I'd love it. But Saturday would be better."

"Alex!" hissed Cindy. Alicia looked at her coolly, and she subsided. The other girls looked dismayed, uncomprehending, though they managed to disguise it by close attention to their food. "Alex, you can't! What if Joe finds out?"

"Joe doesn't own me," she said. "I'm free to do what I want. And what I *don't* want is anyone telling me who I can't go out with."

"Oh, you're right," cried the chubby freshman. "You tell 'em! I wish I had your courage, Alex."

"But Pirella's such a nothing," Sheila said. She'd resolved not to challenge Alex again, but this was too much. Defending him was one thing, but to actually go out with him when everybody knew how Joe hated him, and that Joe was crazy about her . . . nobody but Alex Ryan could even think of doing such a thing. She opened her mouth again, but thought then, *She's doing it just to show that very thing.* That she could. She finished lamely, "But, if you like him, I guess . . ."

"You're right, Alex," said another girl humbly. "We just wish we could do the same things you do."

"For heaven's sake," said Alex, "It's just a movie. Stop acting like he's not human." She felt abruptly sick of her sycophants. "Go to hell, all of you," she snapped. And the table was silent for the rest of the meal.

* * *

The rain stopped after lunch and by three the sun had dried things up pretty well. Phil didn't wait for Anderson to specify his workout. She accepted! And he felt like another try at the Hill.

He kept some plastic cubes of honey in his locker; he opened one and licked out the sweet brown syrup. It left a gluey feel in his dry mouth. *No, it's the Hill that's making me nervous,* he thought. It made his bowels loose too and he attended to that before he went up the steps to the track.

After a good long warmup in the mild sunshine he trotted out Route 158 alone. He had plenty of time before sundown and he went slower than he was used to. He had a long way to go, after all.

It was both harder and easier to run without someone pacing him, as Brentano had the first time. Harder, because he had to set the pace himself; easier, since he could take it slower, as he felt he had to in order to last. He guessed Brentano had gone pretty slow the first time he'd made it the whole way without stopping, though as he toughened up his times would of course decrease.

So he started out slow, almost at a loose jog. His goal today was, first, to get a good workout, and second, to get up the Hill to the top without stopping, in that order. Speed could come later. If he could top out without stopping to rest, he'd be pretty damn tired, no matter how slow he went.

This all ran through his mind. He felt fresh, the air was cool, and the first mile or so was on nearly level ground. Presently he started to think about his date with Alex.

After a while he turned left off the two-lane highway onto what he now saw was named Dawson Road. This led eventually to the smaller hill and over it into the valley beyond.

As he started the upgrade of this hill the first fatigue arrived. *I must be going too slow to feel it this late,* he thought. *I'd better pick it up and get it over with.* He pumped his arm faster and his legs responded and before he'd quite reached the planked bridge he'd broken through the reluctance, pushing harder, but feeling good again. It seemed to be a lot cooler today, perhaps because of the rain the night before. A thin perspiration filmed under his clothes but he felt hardly any on his exposed face and neck.

The straight stretch after the bridge felt good after the climb. He guessed he'd run perhaps four miles so far. But now he was going too fast and he forced his tensed-up body to relax, to stride rather than sprint. He put his head back as he ran, shaking the tension out of his back and shoulders. Then went back to a normal gait, still concentrating on relaxing. *If I can relax while I'm doing something hard,* he thought, *I can keep on doing it for damn near forever.*

The second, steeper hump of the smaller hill came up. He leaned into it, but his legs began to tire, too quickly. They felt heavy and sluggish. He wished he had bigger lungs. His own were suddenly inadequate to supply the air his body demanded. He reached the crest just in time, and staggered over it. *Christ, that was worse than last time,* he thought. *I should have hyperventilated on that straight, built up the oxygen in my blood. Then I could have drawn on it for the steep part.* He had to take advantage of every level and downhill to relax and breathe. That was the only way he was going to get over the Hill. If he ever did.

His legs recovered some on the downhill, but the left one felt tight. He loosened up on it and felt the spasm back off. Shin splints were starting in both the left and right, but he couldn't do anything about that. At least he'd passed the place where the trouble had started Wednesday. *Of course, I'm going a lot slower today.* His throat was dry and as he began to apply the brakes downhill he tried to wet his tongue and swallow.

The honey taste had become disagreeable, changed to something metallic. He spat to the side as he ran and the spittle, viscous from the swift passage of his breath, formed a thread that drooled out far behind before it snapped.

The growl of an engine. He moved to the left of the road. The growl grew louder, then a motorcycle with an anonymously jeaned and leatherjacketed rider screamed past and dove into the valley without slackening. *Oh, shit,* he thought, *now every damn dog in the valley will be awake and laying for me.*

The downward grade began to carry him too fast again and he braked in a little shower of gravel and zigzagged back and forth across the road to keep his speed down. Downhill wasn't effortless, but it was a lot easier than the uphills. He stayed alert for traffic sounds from behind.

As he reached the bottom the horizon contracted from the panorama of farms and fields down to a two-lane asphalt road. The shallow ditches along it were filled with turbid yellow water rushing along nearly at his own pace.

The dogs left him alone for the first half mile but soon he had a little pack of three yelping curs on his heels. Their baying and crying carried out over the fields, and at each farmhouse the chained-up hounds and watchdogs added their howls to mark his passage and encourage his tormentors. A little boy came out on the porch of one house to investigate the commotion. He waved to Phil. Phil waved back with his good arm as he jogged along, one eye on an especially aggressive black dog just behind him.

But they soon tired, or lost interest, and dropped astern as the road curved upward again. He slowed a little more and began panting fast and shallow, charging his bloodstream with oxygen. His legs were tired but they were holding up. The left in particular was going like a champ.

He left the last patch of field behind and the road narrowed again to one lane. It steepened and he put more effort into each step, shortening his stride and breathing more deeply. The air gave out, leaving his lungs fiery. He reached the first switchback and slowly rounded the turn, cutting across it twice to reduce the grade.

The road steepened again. Now each stride was harder and harder, for each had to move his weight not just forward but several inches straight up. His chest heaved. He tried to slow for a second to rest and found himself at a dead stop.

Well, he wouldn't make it today. He panted spasmodically and as he stood there on the road his legs shook. It was just fatigue, though, and if it hurt, it was a clean hurt; he'd run pretty well. The left leg especially had held up beautifully.

He walked back and forth across the road to keep his legs from tightening up and bounced a few times on his toes to stretch the calves. After a few minutes he felt better, but still weak, and his stomach was a vacuum in his gut. He decided to walk the rest of the way up.

Even this was difficult, and he was wheezing when he reached the top. *About six miles to here,* he thought, leaning on the signpost at the crest. Looking out across the valley back the way he'd come, he made out a tiny figure moving steadily down the smaller hill. *Brentano? Better get moving or he'll overtake me.*

He started the long downhill on the far side of Porcupine still wincing at first as his now-cold muscles were stretched again. After a few hundred yards he felt warm again, though, and he finished the long downhill and the three miles of more or less level road back to town with only one five-minute rest.

* * *

Everyone else had finished their workouts and Anderson was leaving the locker room in his street clothes when Phil jogged wearily down the steps. The coach stopped and smiled. "Been out on the Hill, Phil?"

"Yessir, Coach. Nice out there today."

"Make it over?"

"Not quite. Took me two rests. But it went a lot better'n the first time."

"Good.Keep it up." Anderson had started again to leave when a thought occurred. Hadn't he heard some snatch of conversation as students passed in the halls? He turned back. "Pirella, you haven't had any kind of run-in with Joe, have you?"

"Uh, we had some trouble Wednesday, yes. He . . . well, we had some trouble. I'm running alone now."

"This is one school and one team. I expect everybody in cross-country to pull together. We leave personality conflicts and fighting off the track. I'm telling you and I'll remind him of it too. He's a good athlete, but he can be temperamental. So I don't care if you get along on the outside or not, but when you have the red and gold on, you're going to work together. Copy?"

"Well, sir, I didn't do anything. I was only trying – "

"I don't want to hear it," said the older man, picking up his briefcase. "You guys aren't kids any more, to let Mama decide who's right and who's wrong. If you've got a problem and you can't talk it out you can put on the gloves and settle it in the ring. Want me to set it up?"

Phil saw for a moment the red of "crip" and tasted hot tears and hot asphalt again. "Yeah," he said, and was instantly appalled at what he'd done. Brentano had at least fifteen pounds on him and a much longer reach. Not to mention being a mean fighter and having two arms to his one.

"Okay," Anderson said. "I'll talk to him about it. Practice your defense. And I'll be rooting for you, Phil." He left.

"Oh, Jesus," 'Phil said to the empty basement. A single naked bulb burned in the concrete ceiling. He took a super-hot shower and left quickly, before Brentano got back.

As an afterthought he went back and locked the door from the inside so Brentano would have to find the janitor to get his clothes.

SIX

Raymondsville had well-defined places to drink and meet up. For those just past drinking age there was either Willy's or the Hive, bars on the outskirts of town that featured a color scheme to outrage the eyes, a band loud enough to be heard a thousand feet outside the building, and a pushing, thronging, wall-to-wall carpet of teenagers on Friday and Saturday nights. Middle-aged men spent their after-hours time arguing sports and politics and drinking draft beer at the Sherlock Tavern or the Empire State Inn. They never took their wives, and women were rare in these smaller, homelier places.

The older men had the Brown Bear, a not overly clean place with low prices, scarred-up oak booths, and an enormous stuffed bear snarling from the place of honor beside the door.

The twenty-to-thirties congregated at the Pub, the most expensive of the town's holes, but the best in terms of drinks, service and entertainment. The large, dark lounge was veneered with plenty of wood grained plastic, and had the traditional qualities of places that attract human beings in search of their kind; a table-crowded semi-darkness, smoke drifting in layers on the still, warm, humid air, loud music, and easy availability of an inhibition-destroying drug.

On this clear, cool Friday evening, Cheshire's red VW was parked in the Holiday Inn lot, and she was sitting alone at a back table. The evening was young and the band hadn't started up yet, though they were laughing and talking in one of the corner booths.

Cheshire had ordered a martini, her first of the evening, and now she came to the best part. She bit into the olive, savoring the piquant flavor that formed the perfect counterpoint to the dryness of the crystalline liquid, clear and cold as a draft of interstellar space. A waitress slid by and she signaled for another.

She scanned the darkened lounge. Not many guys here tonight. But even fewer single girls. A dark-haired man at the bar, in a gray suit but tieless, glanced her way and she wondered how tall he was.

The band trekked up to the stage. A female vocalist took the mike. The spots went on and the guitarist began tuning up. Bops and crashes from the drummer followed. When they were ready they led off with a mellow number for the couples who were still eating dinner.

The second martini came and it was, if possible, better than the first. "Put it on my tab," she said nonchalantly. The waitress smiled. *Something salty would go with this*, she thought, and was about to ask for chips or popcorn when she remembered her weight. If there was anything that that looked worse than a tall skinny girl it was a tall fat one.

She was finishing that drink when the band started the first dance tune. The dark-haired man kept glancing in her direction. *There's hope for the evening,* she thought gaily. She crossed her legs and held up a finger for the waitress. Another martini? No, she wouldn't be able to dance. "Just make it a ginger ale this time."

"Yes, miss."

The dark-haired man seemed to make up his mind. Draining his glass, he got up and looked in her direction. Feeling a little dizzy, she reminded herself: *Not too friendly at first, now, or he'll get the wrong idea about you.*

* * *

It was five A.M.when Joe coasted to a slow stop in front of the Ryans'. The street was quiet; his engine echoed eerily from house to house. Aside from the street lamps, the porch light at the Ryans' was the only illumination on the block.

He looked over at Alex. She's asleep, he thought fuzzily. His mouth was dry, but his bladder was achingly full. *Too much beer on an empty stomach*, he thought. She opened her eyes as he switched off the engine and he realized she wasn't asleep, only very drunk, drunker than he was.

"Are we home?" she asked in a slurred voice. Her head wobbled and it seemed hard for her to keep her eyes focused on him.

"Yeah," he said. He puthis arm around her again and pulled her to him and she kissed him wetly. He smiled, thinking of the crumpled handkerchief beneath the passenger seat.

He finally broke the kiss. "Kinda late. We better say goodnight. I'll see you Monday at school."

She unfolded herself clumsily from the low car and Joe watched her giggle and reel toward her door. She hadn't gone all the way with him yet, but she had with Fred Barnes, and she would with him too, next time. *She can act so smug and superior at school,* he thought, *but get her alone, give her a drink and she's a slut like all the rest.*

She turned and waved from the porch and he waved back. He rolled off as quietly as he could. He didn't want to wake her folks.

* * *

Phil slept late Saturday morning; he half-awoke several times but stayed under the covers till ten. Nine more hours, he thought, looking at his alarm clock in disgust, to kill 'til I pick Alex up. He wondered what she was doing right now.

At one he was lying on the living-room couch watching Looney Tunes when Jacob came into the living room. Friday night. patrol had kept him out late the night before and he was still sleepy, unshaven, and grouchy. "You 're not going to lie around the house on a sunny day like this, are you?" he demanded.

Phil yawned. Looney Tunes yammered on. "Got any suggestions?"

His step-dad thought, rubbing a hand over his stubble. "Any good games on this afternoon?"

"I checked. Nothing worth watching."

"Well, I can't think of things for you to do," his stepdad said irritably. "I'll be in the workshop most of the day. Got to finish your mom's night table."

"I'll call you if anything promising turns up."

The Three Stooges were on next. They were silly but it would help pass the hours till Alex.

* * *

When Cheshire woke, at a little past eleven, sunlight was flooding across her bed and the sheets were warm to the touch. She had a little headache from mixing drinks the night before at the Pub.

What a waste of time that'd been. A party of four stunning college-age girls had come in after the dancing started and only one man had spoken to her allevening, a balding old drunk who wanted her to buy. She shuddered. How horrible he'd been, touching her knees furtively under the table and whining about his bad luck and his frigid wife.

Her gaze fell on a little bouquet of dried wildflowers on her night table and she smiled. It was nice to see those first thing in the morning. It made the day start so beautifully.

She got up and put on her blue flowered housecoat. She washed her face and brushed her hair and put her makeup on carefully. Then she made herself brunch. It was already noon.

"What shall we do today?" she asked Wolfe idly. He didn't answer. Her list of things to do around the apartment was blank; she'd done them all during the week. Her lesson plans were up to date. Maybe some shopping?

She pulled the VW into a vacant spot on the outskirts of a crowded Toys 'R' Us lot in Hodges, a larger town across the New York line north of Raymondsville. She'd decided to spend her Saturday afternoon shopping for a gift for her sister's little boy.

* * *

Alicia Ryan slept soundly, mouth open a little. Her red hair flowed over the soft pillow like a river of coppered gold. Her room was large and quiet and decorated in blue and white. A haughty-looking angora cat dozed on the slowly ticking register, soaking in the gentle current of heated air. The shades were drawn. Alex did not dream.

* * *

"I don't know why we had to eat so early if your date isn't 'til seven," said Mary irritably. "And you're not going to enjoy your evening very much if you eat so fast. You 're going to get a cramp."

"Mom, I'm really not hungry."

"Philip, you're not listening! I didn't say to eat more. I said

54

not to eat so fast."

"Sorry, Mom." He finished dessert and jumped up from the table. "Anyway, I'm done. Excuse me please, I have to get ready." He left the room.

"What does he have to do?" asked Jake rhetorically. "He doesn't have to shave. Kids don't dress up for dates these days. Don't polish their shoes. Is it just mental preparation, or what?"

"I'm sure I don't know, Jacob," Mary said. "I think he looks fine. But I don't like him going out with the girls at that public school. He's only seventeen."

"Don't worry about that. We had a talk. He knows what to do."

"I don't mean that!" she cried. "Sometimes you say the most horrible things! He's not that kind of boy. But I don't trust those girls."

Upstairs, in the bathroom, Phil was scrutinizing his chin, turning his head from side to side to catch the light. Was that just fuzz? Or the beginning of a beard? *Must be a beard,* he decided. *And it wouldn't hurt to shave.* He went back to his room and found the razor he'd bought that summer. Back at the sink, he studied his face again while the basin slowly filled with steaming water. *Lather?* Jake's was on the shelf. *Guess everything's ready. Here goes.*

He splashed hot water over his face and lathered himself carefully. It was awkward with only one hand, but he managed.

The first stroke. Along the right cheek. So smooth! The blade must be very sharp. Oh, wait. Come to think of it, he hadn't put a blade in yet. He searched the medicine cabinet, found a package of Jake's blades, and borrowed one.

Re-lathering where he'd scraped, he shaved himself very carefully, experimenting with the angle of the blade to the skin. He nicked himself twice, on the neck and on the upper lip. Not good. He finished shaving, washed off, and inspected the results.

The cuts were still bleeding. Tearing out two tiny pieces of toilet paper, he stuck them over the cut, like Jake did. There.

He finished by splashing on some English Leather. It stung. A little more on the neck, on his wrists . . . done. He corked the bottle, put everything away, and headed back to his bedroom.

He took off his jeans and sweatshirt. *What would Alex like me to wear?* Not a tie and jacket. Too dressy for a movie. He tried on several combinations before deciding on dark brown slacks, a yellow short-sleeved shirt, and his red-and-gold track sweater. The long sleeves would hide his left arm, which wasn't a pretty sight in short sleeves. That should be okay . . . He checked the mirror again and noticed that his undershirt, a corner of which was visible at the neck, was frayed. He took everything off again and changed it.

When he was satisfied with his appearance he checked his watch. Almost six. Closing his bedroom door, he reached under his bed and pulled out a gray metal box. He unlocked it and took out an unopened pack of Trojans. *I probably won't be needing these, he thought,* a little guiltily, for Alex was a nice girl; *but if I do, I'd better be prepared.* He tucked the little flat packet into the pocket of the sweater. Finally, he selected a clean white handkerchief out of the pile his mother had ironed for him and placed it carefully over the condoms, wedging them down so they couldn't fall out accidentally.

"Anything else I should take?" he asked his mirror image. He checked his wallet again for money and his ID card. He was ready, then. He checked his watch again. Six o'clock.

His stepdad was calling from downstairs. He shoved the locked box back under his bed, opened his door and bent over the stairwell. "Were you callin' me , Jake?"

"Yeah. Your mom's night table's done. Want to see it?"

"Sure do. Be right· down." He looked at his watch again. Have to call the taxi soon. "On my way down," he called.

"Want a beer, Phil?" his stepdad asked as he came down the stairs into the basement workshop. Jake smelled like he'd had a couple already.

"Sure," said Phil. "Say, that looks nice."

The table *did* look nice. Jake had been given some fresh-cut walnut by one of the other men on the force. He'd let it dry for a year in the attic before cutting, fitting and polishing it into a really fine-looking piece of furniture. "Not a nail or a screw in it," Jake said proudly. "All mortise and tenon joints."

"It looks terrific," said Phil, with honest admiration. He tried the drawer. It slid open smoothly and noiselessly, as if oiled.

Mary came down the stairs with a can of Budweiser and a tall, frosty glass. "Do you want a glass with this, Philip?"

"Yes, thanks, Mom." He poured the beer into the glass and tossed the empty can into the corner wastebasket. *Have to gargle after I drink this*, he thought. *Don't want Alex to smell beer on my breath.*

"Don't drink it too fast," his mother said. She went back upstairs, leaving them together.

"Siddown, Phil." Jake indicated a box with a wave of the polishing cloth, which he was using to bring out a final sheen on the table's surface. "Let's chat a minute. By the way, here's to your date tonight."

"Agreed," Phil said cheerfully. He lifted the tall, cold, suds-topped glass and drank. The tiny bubbles sliced the inside of his throat.

His step-dad took a long pull at his can. "When're you supposed to pick her up, Phil? What's her name, anyway?"

"Alex."

"Alex?" His stepdad sounded doubtful.

"Alicia. She's terrific. I'm taking her to the seven-thirty show."

"Well, say. How you gonna get her there? Gonna walk?"

"I called a taxi for six-forty-five. I'll call to confirm it."

Jake polished away for a moment, intent on the smooth, reflective surface of the walnut. "Cancel it," he said at last. "Take the black and white."

"Oh, no, Jake," Phil said, setting the glass down. "That's town property. What if I banged it up? I'll take the cab. But thanks anyway."

"I think you boys are getting a little drunk. Especially you, Jake," said Mary from the top of the basement stairs.

"Oh, go to hell," Jake said under his breath. He winked heavily at Phil and tossed him a set of keys. "Here. Want my badge and .38 too? They're yours."

"Jacob, you don't know what you're saying," said Mary from upstairs in a horrified tone. "Don't give him a gun!"

Phil jingled the keys in his hand, impressed at their weight. "Well, all right, Dad," he said. "I'll be super careful with it. And I'll have it back before midnight."

Jake took a sip of his beer. *Dad. Is it just because I'm drunk that sounds so good?* "Well, get going," he said gruffly. "Be good, and if you can't be good, be careful." He chuckled at the timeworn joke.

Phil polished off his Straub's and went upstairs. He called and cancelled the cab, rinsed out his mouth, and said goodnight to Mary.

* * *

The squad car started easy. He flicked the lights on, reviewed the controls, and started down the street. It was ten 'til seven.

At five minutes to, a Raymondsville police car pulled quietly to the curb on the 200 block of Revere Street. The engine died and the headlights went out.

Phil sat motionless, eyes on his watch, for four minutes before he turned the courtesy light off and got out. He crossed to an imposing two-story brick home with a huge lawn and an attached two-car garage. When he pressed the lighted bell button a series of mellow chimes sounded deep inside the house. After a few minutes an attractive, auburn-haired older woman answered the door.

"Yes?"

"Hi, I'm Phil Pirella. Alex and I have a date tonight." *She must still be getting ready,* he thought. "Are you her mom?"

"Yes, I'm Mrs. Ryan." But she looked confused. "You have a date with her tonight?"

"Yes, ma'am. For the movie."

"Well, please come in," said Mrs. Ryan, and opened the door.

She disappeared and Phil was left standing uncomfortably in a large, impressively appointed living room. Deep-piled carpet covered the floor. The furniture was heavy antique oak. Leather-bound books were ranked on shelves built into the walls. A grandfather clock ticked deliberately in a shadowy alcove. The slow ticking made him realize how quiet the house was.

Alex's mom returned, with a glass of milk and a large plate of English cookies. "Alex will be down in just a few minutes." She smiled. "She's just getting ready. Won't you sit down and have some cookies while you wait?"

"Thanks." He sat and tried a cookie. They were dainty but good.

Mrs. Ryan sat gracefully on the edge of a large sofa and smiled at him when he looked up from the cookies. She pulled her skirt down a little and Phil thought, *She has nice legs.* She also had a very nice smile.

"Alicia didn't mention she had a date tonight, Bill. Where did you say you were going?"

"Phil," said Phil. "Just to the movie downtown. It's science fiction. I think."

"It sounds terrific . . . Phil." She smiled again.

He stole a look at the clock and then at his own Timex. Seven-twenty.

"Hi, Phil."

He rose as she came down the stairs. She was lovely in a green pleated skirt and a cream cashmere pullover. Her smile lit the room.

Not bad for a housecoat and slippers ten minutes ago, thought her mother. But aloud she said brightly, "Now don't stay out too late, kids. Bring her home early, Phil, she needs her beauty sleep. And have fun, both of you. Goodnight."

* * *

Alex laughed when she saw the squad car. "Are you kidding? We're going in this? I've never ridden in one of these before "

"My dad let me have it for the evening," he said nonchalantly. He opened the door for her and as she got in her hair brushed against his arm, sending a strange sensation up his backbone. He saw a flash of her legs by the courtesy light before the door closed. He went around the front and got in the other side.

"Where are we going tonight? I've forgotten."

"A movie. An adaptation of an old H. G. Wells story."

"Sounds terrific," she said enthusiastically. Her scent filled the car. He· stole a glance. She was looking at him with wide, dancing eyes and a smile that reminded him of her mother's.

"You look really lovely tonight," he said.

"You look nice, too. Is that a cross-country sweater?"

"Um, not exactly. Track. I ran, um, I ran middle distance last year." Not exactly true, but close.

She sat back. "Well, shall we go?"

"Oh, sure," he said hastily. He was relieved when the car started on the first try.

She bent forward again. "What's that on your lip, Phil?"

"What?"

"There's something on your lip."

Sickening realization struck and he yanked the tissue off, roughly, and felt his upper lip start to bleed again. *Oh, Jesus,* he thought in despair, *How I wish I had two hands.* He dabbed at the cut with his handkerchief while Alex stared in silence out of the window at her neighbors' homes. At last he felt he'd staunched the bleeding and he put the squad car in Drive and pulled into the street.

Alex still sat quietly. She was looking straight ahead now and as he stole a glance at her he could see her silhouette against the window. "It's, um, a nice night," he said.

"Yes, it is."

He turned down Pershing Avenue and they soon reached Main. He parked the black-and-white in the shadow of a tree a block away from the theater. "There's more parking in front," she said.

"Well . . . I don't want to get my old man in trouble," Phil said. "He really shouldn't have let me take this car. But it'll be okay as long as I don't advertise it's me driving it."

"I see," she said.

The feature had already started when they got to the theater. They felt their way up the aisle, Alex in front, while the credits unrolled on the screen. The Grand was the only theater in Raymondsville, and tonight it was packed. They finally found seats near the front and climbed over several people to get to them. Alex bent to place her purse under her seat.

The seats were close together, with only a narrow wooden armrest separating them, and at first he was acutely conscious of her sitting next to him. But as the show progressed he became more and more absorbed in it. He'd read the original story and couldn't help noticing what they'd changed. The story line was the same, except for a more overt love interest, but he doubted the technology was what Wells had had in mind.

Midway through the movie he felt a light touch on his shoulder.When he turned his head his cheek brushed her hair. It smelled good. Her head was leaning, very gently, against his shoulder. He put his good right arm gently around her but she didn't move after that till the end when the lights came on.

"That was a good movie," he said. They were walking along Main Street, back toward the car, and the air was still and cold. The moon was up, just a sliver of it, and it hung low ahead of them, just over the First Raymondsville Bank building.

"Thanks for taking me, Phil."

He glanced at her. She was hugging herself and looked cold.

"Are you cold? Why don 't you take my sweater?"

"Oh, I couldn't," she began, but he had it off already. She looked at his bare left arm, then away quickly. "You're very considerate, Phil."

He felt warm inside, even without the sweater. The air was chilly, though, and he was glad when they reached the car. It was cold inside and the seats were clammy so he turned on the heater. Thank God it was clean, his stepdad complained about the drunks barfing in the back seat when he had to take them in.

"Want to drive around a little? We can stop in at the Pub for a drink if you want."

"Oh, gee, I'd love to," she said, "but I'm a little tired tonight. I don't know why. Why don't we just go back to my house and have a glass of wine or something?"

That sounded promising. He started the engine, peered up and down the street for other cop cars, then moved out into the Saturday night traffic. The other vehicles made room respectfully for the black-and-white.

The porch light at her house was on, but the place was quiet when they went in. Phil looked at the time and was surprised to see it was ten already.Her dad and mom must go to bed early. Either that or the house was so large you couldn't tell if anyone else was home. Had there been lights on upstairs when they pulled in? He couldn't remember.

A candle was burning on a small table near the window and the scent from it pervaded the large dim room. "Please, sit down," Alex said. She draped his sweater over a chair and disappeared into the kitchen.

He hesitated, then sat down on the same couch Mrs. Ryan had used, draping his arm suggestively over the back of it. The old clock chimed softly ten times and then resumed its measured ticking.

He couldn't help comparing this large, dignified room with the shabby little lived-in one at his house. It took both money and good taste to furnish a room like this. Ryan, he thought. I wonder if her dad's the Ryan who's the chairman of the plywood plant.

His thoughts were interrupted by Alex'ss triumphant return bearing two goblets filled with sparkling pink wine. She set them on a low table before the couch. "Wait a min before you start," she smiled, and was back quickly with a bowl of corn chips. "I missed dinner."

"Oh, I didn't know. We could have had a snack downtown."

"I try to avoid those ptomaine palaces as much as I can."

They laughed together and he felt suddenly that there was an intimate air in the room that hadn't been there before. She curled up on the sofa beside him and lifted her glass to the candlelight. They clinked classes and he sipped, gaze on her face and the curve of her arm. Her eyes were distant, seemingly focused on the candle, which burned steadily in a long tongue of light. The wine tasted sour but seemed to have a kick to it if the warm ball it formed in his stomach was any indication. "This wine's pretty good," he said.

"Dad knows a lot about wine."

Again it was quiet. The candlelight threw rosy shadows on her face and hid her face in mystery. The room was very still except for the tick of the old clock and the thump of his heart. She was sitting back with her shoes kicked off and her legs half tucked under her. His eyes found it very easy to follow the gentle curves from her neck down the fuzzy cashmere sweater and half-revealed legs. He liked her little toes. She noticed his glance and tucked her feet the rest of the way under her.

He tried, "Um, what kind is it?"

"The wine? Oh, I didn't notice. Something from Portugal, or Spain, I think."

She raised her glass again for another sip. *She's so pretty. Does she want me to kiss her? Is this the time?*

Alex was thinking, too. *I'll let him finish his wine, then ease him out. God, what a dull evening.* Well, last night made up for it in advance. Maybe she was letting Joe go too far too fast, but he was so aggressive, and he really knew how to turn her on.

She turned her head and smiled at Phil over her glass. *I forgot all about promising to see him tonight,* she thought. *But I went out with the crippled boy when the whole rest of the school was down on him.* It had certainly put that bitch Conrad in her place. It would give Joe something to think about when he heard about it, too. Though he wouldn't get jealous of a nobody like Pirella.

Her lips are redder than the wine, Phil thought dizzily. What did a woman's lips taste like, anyway? The tip of her tongue showed for an instant. He slid his arm down to touch her shoulders. "This is a nice room," he said.

"Mom redecorated last year. I helped with the drapes and some of the furniture."

64

"It looks great. Are these antiques?"

"Oh, no." She laughed, amused at his ignorance. "It's all new. Solid oak, from Dunlop 's in North Carolina. The clock's the only the only old thing here. Dad's family brought it from Ireland when they came over. It's the only real heirloom we have from his side of the family."

There was silence again and it grew until Phil could make out her breathing. She was leaning back, looking very relaxed, her hair falling over the back of the sofa. She seemed to be thinking about something. *Or maybe she's waiting for me to kiss her.*

She'd been thinking about Joe, but she caught his lean in and thought, *I believe he wants to kiss me. Well, why not, poor kid, I can be his first.* She turned her face and closed her eyes, keeping her mouth firmly closed.

His heart was thundering in his ears. He leaned forward even more and met her lips. They felt . . . rubbery . . . and, cool, and . . . .

Dizzy with success, he put his right hand on her breast.

She recoiled across the sofa as if she'd been touched by some unclean thing. Pushing him violently away, she wiped her mouth, eyes blazing. "You animal," she hissed. "Keep your filthy hands to yourself. I'm nice enough to go out with you and you. . . . . "

He lowered his still outstretched hand. "I thought – "

"Just wait 'til I tell Joe what you tried to do to me," she said. Her face was losing its initial expression of shock, becoming a white mask of loathing. "They warned me what kind of a creep you are. But I tried to be kind." She threw the dregs of her wine into his burning face. "Get out of my house, you filthy little defective."

Without thinking, he slapped her. Then froze, mind reeling with combined rage and dismay. Her mouth was open with shock for a moment, her cheek reddened with the blow.

And then she screamed, and the scream echoed in the void

of his mind until only one thought remained: *flight*. He staggered up, stumbled over the coffee table, spilling his own wine on the carpet, and ran toward the door as she screamed again.

The night air galvanized him and he ran down the sidewalk to the squad car and unlocked it as quickly as his shaking hand would permit. Behind him, in the house, lights came on and a man's figure appeared at the door. The cruiser's engine, still warm, caught and he gunned it, too hard, and the car shuddered slowly down the drive. He released the parking brake with a curse and it leapt into the street, tires squealing. He hauled the wheel hard to avoid the line of parked cars on the opposite side of the street. But not hard enough. Metal scraped and squalled as the squad car's fender slid along the flank of a light-colored sedan.

Then he was clear and he realized through the numbness that his headlights were still off. Stabbing them on, he tromped the pedal hard and the powerful V8 took him by the shoulders and pressed. him firmly back into the seat. A roar filled the street and the speedometer needle jumped to sixty.,

He eased off on the accelerator only when the intersection loomed and he slowed and turned right onto Maple. He didn't think about where he was going. For the moment he was just fleeing, and the only thing that counted was the distance he could put between himself and the blunder he'd just made.

Before he realized it he was out of town and tearing along 158. The motor was howling, but he was afraid to take his eyes from the narrow tunnel of light down which he was hurtling to look down at the speedometer. Gravel rang and pinged against the bottom of the car as the wheels brushed the berm.

He caught sight of the left turn off the two-lane at the edge of his headlights and jammed the brakes. They were power brakes, police duty, and he almost went through the windshield, but he held to the wheel and spun it hard left. Then he was in the one-lane and beginning to climb in the darkness. Trees blotted out the stars but he wasn't looking up. He stepped down harder and the cruiser lunged up the steepening grade.

He drove hard and didn't think about anything. Just concentrated on staying on the narrow road. His wheels slid off the pavement at seventy and he nursed them back on in a cold sweat. He realized the danger but didn't lessen the pressure of his foot on the accelerator.

The plank bridge clattered for an instant under the heavy car and was gone. He took the straight stretch at eighty and braked savagely into a power skid around the corner. The smaller hill slowed the powerful car hardly at all and its crest rose swiftly and he was going so fast as he shot over that the car rose slightly against its suspension as if to take off. He let it out going down into the nightfilled valley and the needle rose steadily 'til it topped a hundred. No dog had a chance to do more than raise its head before he thundered past and dwindled into the shattered night.

He was forced to slow when he reached the Hill, not from the grade, at first, but because of the closeness of the switchbacks and the narrow, ditch-lined road. When he cleared the hairpin turns and began the curving climb toward the summit the car felt logy for the first time. He had the pedal all the way to the floor and still the engine labored, the transmission downshifted, and his speed dropped first to forty and then to twenty.

At last he topped the summit and the valley lay before him. He pulled off at the overlook and parked next to the sign. *I'd better let it cool off a while after that climb,* he thought, and turned the engine and headlights off.

It was very quiet then and presently the engine block began to tick slowly as hot metal began to contract in the cold air. It reminded him of the grandfather clock in the Ryans' home.

He looked at the dashboard clock. It was only ten-twenty.

EIGHT

By Sunday evening, most of the circle – and it was a large one – of Alex's friends had heard her tragic tale, and each had done her best to calm her; but to no avail. Over the telephone she sounded wild, frightened, deeply shocked and hurt by the unsuspected brutality of someone she'd trustingly accepted and championed.

By Monday the story had spread through the school like summer wildfire. The teachers were puzzled at the surreptitious whispering and note-passing. Normally on Monday mornings the students sat in depressed silence. Now, in the corridors, the whispers swelled into a loud buzz. The girls were voluble; the boys were quieter, as they clustered in knots of three and four, discussing what had happened and what should be done.

Phil wasn't there Monday. Mary had phoned the main office to report he was feeling sick and wouldn't be in. The main office secretary remembered he hadn't missed a single day all sophomore year, so she didn't ask for a note.

His absence was a mistake. He was being judged, as surely as if he were sitting before a courtroom. And there was no attorney for the defense. Alex was wonderful in the role of assaulted, and nearly martyred, purity. His absence was taken as proof of her story. By that afternoon all the potsherds had been collected. The verdict was guilty, the penalty, ostracism.

Only Carl Saarlo and Myrna Hastings abstained. Myrna, timid though she was, ventured to say that if anything had really happened, it was probably Alex who'd invited it. For that she was set on by Cindy Robaley and two other girls, her face scratched and her glasses broken. She was left weeping. Carl put it more bluntly: "I don't believe a word. Pirella'd never dare even to kiss her. She made it all up." This was received by the locker room with nothing more than silent disapproval. Saarlo was short but he didn't put up with much.

At lunch Brentano heard the whole story, and as Alex blushed at some of the words she had to use, he trembled with outrage.

When last period ended, Sheila Conrad joined the little knot of girls gathered protectively around Alex at her locker. She pushed a sophomore out of her way and put an arm around Alex's bowed shoulders. Ryan looked haggard and woebegone.

"Are you feeling better, Alex, dear?" Sheila asked gently.

"Oh, a little, Sheila. I'll be all right."

"Have you told the police, honey?"

"I thought about it, but I decided not to. His father's a cop. They'd just make it look as if . . . as if I were the bad one. No, I'll just try to forget it happened."

"Oh, Alex. You're so brave." Sheila hugged her close.

The girls murmured sympathetically and reached out to touch the former rivals. Finally Sheila shook Alex encouragingly and let her go. Smiling sadly, Alex turned back to her locker and began to put her books away. The others drifted off, many of the younger ones with tears in their eyes. Would they be able to bear up if they'd such an experience? One only a woman could have, or could understand.

Saarlo called Phil that night. After several rings someone picked up. "Phil's sick in bed," a woman said.

"Mrs. Pirella, this is Carl, his friend," Saarlo said hastily, before she could hang up. "See if he'll come to the phone for me. Tell him it's important."

"Well, wait a minute. I'll see." After a while she came back on. "He'll be down to in a minute."

Finally he came on. "Carl?"

"Yeah. You really sick today?"

"Um, yeah. Got a bad cold."

"You sound okay."

"Well, I'm not. What did you want, Carl?"

"I won't pull any punches. You're in trouble. It's Alex Ryan."

"I thought I might be."

"She says you tried to rape her Saturday night."

"Oh, God. I only tried for a feel."

"Not what she's saying, buds."

There was silence on the line, then "Whatever else she's saying isn't true."

"Hey I believe you. I stuck up for you, but everybody else is out for your head. You comin' in tomorrow?"

"I don't know. Should I?"

"No. I'll tell your side. What really happened. Nobody's heard that yet. That's all that happened, right? You went for her tit?"

"Yeah.Well, no. I, um, slapped her."

A pause. Then, "She slapped you?"

"No. I slapped her. She called me a . . . well, she called me a name."

Another pause. "You slapped her because she wouldn't let you feel her tit?"

"No, because of what she called me. I lost it, I shouldn't have done it. But I didn't try to rape her. All I got was a kiss. Then everything sort of . . . went to shit from there."

Saarlo was silent for a second more. Then, "Well, I'll tell 'em that. But you better lay out for a couple days. Let it blow over."

71

"Okay, thanks for calling. You're a good friend."

Phil hung up and went back up to his room. He had to think about what to do next. He wished he had somebody he could ask for advice. But he couldn't think of anybody.

* * *

Cheshire had heard the murmurings in her class and in the halls, and had missed Phil in class, but she didn't get the full story until noon break. At the teacher's table, though, she sat next to Martha Carzie, a student teacher who seemed to enjoy an unparalleled rapport with the kids, possibly because she looked like a senior herself. Martha was telling the story to Reba, the head secretary. Cheshire was appalled. She could have believed something like that of the backseats jobies in her classes, but Phil?

"Do you really believe what you're saying?" she asked Carzie.

The younger teacher considered. "It's all over the school," she said slowly. "But it does all hang on the word of just the Ryan girl. And no one's heard from the boy yet."

"Could Alicia be making it up for some reason?"

"I don't know her that well," said Mrs. Carzie cautiously, "but why would she want to?"

"Do you know of any grudge she had against Phil?"

"Who's Phil?"

"Pirella. The boy she's accusing."

"Oh. I didn't know his name. Well, yes, in a way. She's involved with Joe Brentano, and I hear the boys were in a fight or something at track practice last week."

"Could she be trying to manipulate them?"

"I guess it's possible. But she seemed really upset in class today. She's really too young to practice such . . . duplicity, I guess?"

"Oh, you've seen the way she dominates that little clique of hers. Don't tell me she's too young, Martha."

Well, perhaps," said Mrs. Carzie. "But really, Cheshire, you're being awfully defensive."

"Well, we haven't even heard his side of the story. That's all I'm trying to say: his side hasn't been heard yet, and it should be before everyone decides he's a, a sex criminal."

"I can't fault that. But the longer he stays away the more difficult it will be to get any kind of fair hearing."

"I just can't see him doing anything like that," Cheshire said. "Although I admit I've never seen him outside of class."

"Who Knows," intoned little Mrs. Carzie solemnly, "What Evil Lurks in the Hearts of Men. Especially teen-aged ones."

Cheshire laughed. "You may be right. He may be a one-handed Jack the Ripper. But somehow I can't believe little Alicia Ryan's as wholesome and blameless as she wants us to think."

* * *

When Jake came home that afternoon Mary was mending a pair of socks in front of *Days of our Lives*. He threw his uniform cap on the couch and unbuckled his gun belt. The holster was empty, and the bright nickeled .38 cartridges were absent from the loops on the worn black leather belt.

"Damn this town," he said, to no one in particular.

His wife looked up in surprise. "You're home early. Is something wrong?"

"Everything travels so fast," he mumbled. "And everyone knows everybody else's business. Goddamned busybodies."

"Well, sit down and tell me. I'll get you a beer, you look hot."

He collapsed into the recliner with a sigh. "I tried to tell Chief Bradner I did it myself, chasing a speeder. He listened 'til I was through, then said he had heard a different story. The Ryan girl's spread it all over town Phil tried to . . . well, attack her."

"Oh." Mary set down the tray she was holding and put both hands to her mouth. "Our boy wouldn't –"

"I know, I don't believe he'd do such a thing either. But apparently a lot of other people do."

"Was Chief Bradner angry you told him the story about the speeder?"

"Yeah, I guess, but he was a lot madder about me loanin' the car out in the first place. He called it a flagrant misuse of Town property, and a failure to use good judgement."

"What's he going to do?"

"Well, for starters, now the cruiser stays at the station overnight. I'll have to get a ride in with Eric in the morning. He's not going to suspend me, but he said he considered it. Seriously. Instead, he's going to withhold the report to the insurance company and I'm to pay for the damage to both cars. Of course, if it happens again, I'm toast, as far as the department's concerned."

She looked worried. "How much will the repairs be?"

"Well, it won't be a small amount, hon, but it's within our means. We've got it in the savings account. And I can moonlight as a guard at the plywood plant to get the rest. You won't need to scrimp."

"Oh, but I can cut down some more. I have a little I kept back, too, if you want it. Working two jobs is awful hard, Jake."

"Don't worry about me." He kissed her cheek. "We'll pull through. But don't cut down any more on the groceries. I'm still a growin' boy, remember?" He patted her and went into the bedroom to change.

Her eyes fell on the empty holster. "What happened to your gun, Jake?"

His voice came hollowly out from the bedroom. "Another of Bradner's little precautions. I have to leave it at the station now after work. Afraid I'll loan it to somebody, I guess."

He laughed, but it was a humorless sound.

* * *

Phil had been lying in bed upstairs, listening to every word Jake and Mary said. Hearing his stepdad had to suffer for his screwups didn't lighten his depression. *I wish I'd never asked her out*, he thought miserably. How had he been so stupid as to try for a feel? But he hadn't tried to rape her. He couldn't believe what Carl had said, that she was saying that in school.

Brentano had done that too, taking something stupid he'd done and blowing it out of all proportion. Why did people have it in for him? Was it just because he limped, had a useless arm, had grown up on crutches? They ought to feel sorry for him, not hate him.

Should he go in tomorrow? Or take Saarlo's advice, stay out longer and let him tell Phil's side of the story? He meant well, but maybe the longer he stayed out, the more they'd think he was really guilty. It'd be hard enough trying to pit his word against the most popular girl in school, but if he stayed away, suspicion would harden into certainty.

Jake had said something like that once. If the cops suspected someone of larceny, or some other non-violent crime, the police would let him find out, indirectly, that he was under suspicion. If he left town or went under cover when he heard he was being watched, they knew he was probably guilty, and would concentrate on finding a witness or evidence to go to court with.

He decided to go in tomorrow. He'd confront Alex, and probably that meant Brentano too. He'd say he was sorry, and tell everyone what really happened, without trying to cover up the blunder he'd made. But he had to set the record straight: he'd never thought of going any farther, never thought of using

75

force.

If only he hadn't slapped her . . . most of the kids would think the worst. But hiding just wasn't going to do it. Decision made, he got out of bed, put on his PJ bottoms, and went downstairs.

* * *

"How are you feeling? Is your cold any better?"

"Lots. I think I'll be able to go back to school tomorrow."

His mother was looking at him with searching eyes. She probably wanted to ask him, *did you?* To be reassured he hadn't. But she only turned away. "Well, don't go in unless you're sure you're better."

His stepdad came in from the back porch. 'Phil," he said tonelessly, in the voice he used for traffic offenders. "Like to talk to you alone. Mary, you mind?"

"I was just going to start dinner." She put her darning away and went into the kitchen and closed the door.

"Sit down," his stepdad said. Phil sat on the sofa, expecting the worst. It was the tone Jake had used when he had a spanking coming. He didn't think that was what was happening here, though he kind of wished it would. Simple, and quickly over.

"I wasn't real happy with the accident last night, but I was pleased you came to me and admitted it like a man. But since then I've heard some things that suggest maybe you didn't tell me everything that happened Saturday night." Jake waited, then, "Do you know what I'm talking about, Phil?"

"Yeah. Yes, sir."

"Well?"

"Well, like, Carl Saarlo called me and told me what she's been saying in school. I didn't try to attack her, or anything, Jake. All I did was, um . . . touched her breast."

76

"Through her clothes, you mean?" Phil nodded. "And that's all?"

"That's all, Dad, I swear. I didn't do another goddamn thing. Anything sexual, I mean. But I um, lost my temper."

"There's no need to swear, Phil."

"Sorry."

"And, what?"

"Sir?"

"You said, you lost your temper. And then what?"

"Um, I slapped her."

"Shit," his stepdad said. Then was silent for several seconds. At last he spoke, slowly. "Phil, I'm on your side. I kind of have to stick up for you, and by God I would, even if you were in the wrong. I believe you're telling the truth. The whole time I've known you, you never told me a lie, even when it would have saved you a whipping. You better be damned glad you never did, because that's the main reason I believe you now.

"So that's settled, and if anyone outside school says anything against you, he'll have to answer to me."

"Thanks, Jake," Phil said, vastly relieved.

"Inside the school is your problem. I can't help you there; I'd do you more harm than good."

"Yeah.Probably."

They were both silent. Then Jacob reached out and punched his stepson on the leg. "And don't worry about the car. The insurance'll cover that."

"Thanks, Dad. Having you and mom believing me makes a lot of difference."

For the first time since Saturday night he began to feel good inside.

NINE

The next morning dawned clear and warm. As he dressed to jog in to school Phil listened to the weather report on tv. Mostly clear, cooler with the possibility of showers toward evening. *I'll have to look again this afternoon, but today might be the time to try the Hill again.*

He ate a light breakfast, tea and two pieces of toast with jam, so his stomach wouldn't be upset by the jog in. At last he started out, running very slowly in the coolness of dawn because he didn't have time in the mornings to warm up properly.

He entered school though the locker room, avoiding the mob streaming in though the main doors. The buses would start to arrive and the corridors would be jammed.

The gymnasium was empty, though, and he was glad for that. Actually, he was getting pretty good at changing in and out of running clothes without help. It was quiet at the lockers without boys shouting and showers going but he could hear, above his head, how the halls were filling. The distant murmur that filtered down through the concrete ceiling was like the somnolence of a monster that, once aware of his presence, would demand blood. Fear writhed in his stomach. *How will they act*, he wondered. *Will they let me explain, will they listen? What will they do to me?* He finished buttoning his shirt and stood at the door out, afraid to open it.

He pictured a series of possible scenes when he walked in: a spontaneous, angry attack by the crowd, like the riots on television; a challenge by Brentano, man to man, in the corridor?

Whatever happened, he'd stand and fight. There'd be no lickspittle apologies for something he hadn't done.

When he finally walked up the terrazzo steps to the main hallway, he was pleasantly surprised. The chatter and noise were interrupted by silence, which spread by a ripple movement to the length of the locker-lined hall. Heads turned toward where he stood, then away

With the same peristaltic movement the murmur resumed. He sighed, relieved. *They aren't going to tear me apart, at least,* he thought.

He began to limp down the middle of the hall, letting the door swing to behind him. As it clicked he felt like an early saint entering the Coliseum. The first kids he passed didn't react. *Carl was wrong,* he thought. *It's not all over the school. They don't care that much. I can fight it.*

He walked the length of the hall to his locker unnoticed and unmolested. No one so much as frowned at him. Actually, no one even looked as he passed. He grinned to himself. He opened his locker and glanced over at Steve Rapisjek. "Hi, Steve," he said cheerfully, though even at best he usually only got a grunt in reply.

His teammate didn't seem to hear him. He was busy deep in his locker. After a moment he clanged the door shut and walked away. *Must not have heard me,* Phil thought.

He pulled out the books for that morning's classes. Four hardcover textbooks and two notebooks, a heavy load for a guy with only one arm that worked. But he could manage. He closed the locker and spun the dial.

He walked into Senora Antonez's classroom as first period bell rang, settled into his seat, and stuffed his books under the desk top. This was the only classroom that still had the ancient flip-top desks. He opened *El Camino Real,* the Spanish textbook. "So begins another exciting day of learning," he asided to Greg

Allemand with a grin. Allemand, a thin studious boy with fine ash-blond hair, was looking through his textbook. He didn't seem to hear him.

"Greg," Phil said. "Hey, Greg?"

Allemand just kept riffling through the pages, and Phil realized he wasn't going to answer. He turned in near panic to the student behind him, a shy Black girl he knew only slightly. "Hey, Gloria," he said. She dropped her eyes and didn't answer.

By the end of second period he got it. He was silenced. The other kids, pointedly ignoring him in the halls, saw him go back to his locker before Senior English, slam his books into it, and claw out some others, he didn't seem to care which. One fell at his feet. They watched as he kicked at it savagely and missed; the tinny clang as his foot struck metal echoed through the hall. But no one appeared to notice.

* * *

When Pirella came in Cheshire was glad for a moment he'd decided to come back. But when he slammed his books on his desk so hard the classroom echoed, she was shocked. This wasn't the studious, well-behaved boy she was used to. She started to walk toward him, but one of the girls interposed herself. "Don't talk to him, Miss Marzeau," she said in a low voice, and walked on to her seat.

Cheshire stopped, hesitated, and then went back behind her desk.

Phil was seated now, head in his hands, eyes turned inward, denying the existence of the outside world. *So that's their answer*, she thought. *Outlaw him without a trial, destroy his self-respect.* She looked at Alex, sitting stiffly with head turned ostentatiously away from his direction, a look of suffering innocence on her face. Cheshire hated her. There had to be something she could do.

But while she thought, a class waited to be taught. She'd start as usual for now.

"Good morning, class. How many of us completed the reading today? Ok, good. Then we can get into discussing Jim's success in Patustan."

Phil kept his head and eyes down for the rest of class. He'd had enough of meeting other students' furtive glances, seeing their eyes go distant and slide off as if he was nothing more than an obstacle to clear vision. A nonperson. He remembered the James Baldwin book they'd read last year. The looks Baldwin described whites giving non-whites, how they looked at something the existence of which was not to be noticed or admitted.

But for the most part his thoughts weren't that clear. He kept searching for a word for this emotion. Dread? Resentment? Inferiority? Shit, it was working. He'd give in, he'd admit anything just to be talked to a gain. How long could he take this? And how long did they plan to keep it up? Until graduation? Until he went crazy? Maybe if he apologized to her. In public. A public apology, yeah. But for what? And would she listen? If he approached her in the hall, or at lunch, what if she screamed? They'd beat him up, stomp him, maybe kill him.

Shit, and what about Brentano? By now Anderson would have passed on his challenge. Well, a bloody nose would be better than this.

He kept on mulling it over, feeling more and more depressed, and at last got sick of thinking about it. He decided to try the Hill again that afternoon. Exercise always made him feel better, especially after a long hot shower and a brisk toweling. And during the run he could forget everything else. Yeah . . . now if the weather would only cooperate.

The Hill

* * *

Alex was eating quietly with her gang, the usual chatter subdued today, when Brentano came up to the table. Sheila slid over to make room.

"How you doin'?" he asked, putting his arm around Alex.

"I'm feeling a little better, Joe."

Sheila said hotly, "It's just a shame, he's just walking around, cool as you please, and we can't do anything."

He smiled grimly. "Don't worry about that. Coach set me up to fight him tomorrow."

"Your coach? What's he got to do with it?"

"He doesn't know about what he did to Alex," Joe said. "He thinks it's some kid's beef and he wants it fixed for the team. So he set us up for boxing."

"And you 're going to beat him up? That'd be better than this silly silencing."

"Oh, you can't hurt anybody with those fifteen-ounce gloves on. And if I really tried to, Anderson'd stop me."

Sheila frowned. "So . . . how?"

He looked away. "I think it'd be better if you guys didn't know."

* * *

Phil suited up in the locker room, not bothering to ask for a hand. The other runners seemed more reluctant about the silencing, but he wasn't about to hand them a chance to cut him. He pulled his left arm out almost straight, gasping at the pain, and, holding it against his left leg, pulled the sleeve on quickly. The trousers were easier.

He jogged up the steps, through the aluminum-framed doors, and out into an overcast, threatening, cool afternoon.

He was well into his warmup when Anderson walked over from where he'd been talking to Ray Corrigan. "Pirella. Remember that talk we had about you and Brentano?"

"Yes, sir."

"We spoke yesterday. He seemed glad to get the whole thing out in the open and cleared up."

"Yes, sir, so do I," said Phil. *Does Anderson know about this latest thing with Ryan? No, I guess not.* "When and where, sir?"

"Tomorrow, after last period, in the ring under the gym. I'll make sure it's a fair fight and nobody gets seriously hurt."

"Thanks for setting this up, Coach."

"Well, I can't let interpersonal conflicts tear up the team. It's part of the job. By the way, I've arranged one other thing. Actually, he suggested it. He'll go in the ring with one arm. Like you. He won't use his left."

"That makes it more even, I guess."

"Well, he still has weight and reach," said the coach. "But as far as guts go, you're even. Don't go in that ring with the idea that you're going to lose. Just keep your head, and apply what you learned in gym. And fight clean."

"Will the other guys be there, Coach?"

"No. This is a grudge fight, not a boxing smoker. No kibitzers . . . running the Hill again?"

"Gonna try, sir."

"Well, go to it." Anderson turned away.

Phil looked skyward. It was getting rapidly darker, and a moisture-laden wind began to blow. He went back inside and put his windbreaker on over his sweatshirt before he started down Maple Street.

Two cars, both with headlights on, passed as he hit the grade climbing up Route 158 out of town. He left the sidewalks behind and passed the few new suburban-style homes dotting the sides of the road. Then he was in the countryside. He topped the slight rise and started down, staying off the hard asphalt as much as he could. The wind, from directly ahead on this leg, buffeted him and roared in his ears. *Well, it's keeping my hair out of my eyes. Gee, it's getting cold. Hope it holds off raining another hour. Maybe I need one of those knit caps the other guys wear in the winter.* He could ask his mom to knit him one.

As he ran on it was easier to forget his troubles. How could he feel depressed when he felt so strong, so young, so eager to run?

He passed the first valley and after a few hundred yards turned into the wooded one-laner. The trees, crowding almost into the road, cut the wind and he ran more easily without its buffeting, but it was still cold. The air was moist and heavy in his throat. He remembered reading about electrical charges in the air just before thunderstorms. *Is that why I feel so good now? Whatever, I'm glad I came out. Even if it rains, it's better than stewing in my room.*

The narrow road curved and began a gradual, graceful rise. *The woods are lovely, dark and deep, But I have promises to keep.* Robert Frost, from Junior English. He smiled.

The cramp struck without warning. He felt his calf stiffen slightly, took four or five strides, and it suddenly knotted. The agony was intense. He bent and gripped it, gasping. The twisted lump of muscle, contracted to a rocklike hardness, jumped and quivered in his hand. The pain forced him to the ground and he lay on his side, panting, pounding at it with his fist, digging his fingers into it. *Relax,* he thought furiously. *Jeez.* Seizing the toe of his shoe, he pulled itupward to stretch the calf.

It softened a bit, then reextended itself as suddenly as it had cramped. He worked the foot up and down to keep it stretched, not letting it re-tense. *A long time since I had one that bad,* he thought. *Since track season last year.*

He kept massaging it. As his other muscles cooled they too began signaling tautness and soreness to his brain. After a few more minutes his calf felt good enough he could get up again. He tried to jog a few steps, but the warning tension returned after a few strides. Stopping immediately, he massaged it again.

Shit, he thought, *guess that's it for today.* Disappointment at not being able to run farther was strangely mixed with the body's lazy relief at not having to run farther. *Have to walk back. I should have worn two pairs of pants, or run a shorter workout at a faster pace.*

He was limping back, was halfway back down the gentle hill with the mysterious dark woods, when Brentano came around the turn. His lanky form was enveloped in layers of gray sweats, with a red and gold knit cap and gloves.

He slowed as he recognized Pirella. "Quittin' early, crip? Got plans to grope somebody else's girl tonight?"

"Can it," Phil said, keeping his voice steady, but only with an effort. Was the guy going to hammer him right here, away from anybody watching? It would be a golden opportunity. "We'll get it settled in the ring tomorrow."

"We'll settle it, all right. But not with padded gloves and a ref to make sure nobody gets messed up. It's past that, creep."

"What're you talking about?"

"Forget the ring. Under the grandstand, tomorrow, same time. Bring a friend, if you can find one. And a blade. A nice sharp shiny blade."

"No," Phil said, back-jogging away.

"Fight me with a knife tomorrow, or being silenced will be fun compared to what we 'll do." The senior spat on the ground.

Phil didn't respond, and after a moment Brentano picked up his pace again and loped off. "Tomorrow, Pirella," floated back on the cold wind, then he was over the crest and gone.

Phil resumed walking back slowly. The breeze, blowing from behind him now, hurried him along, buffeting him about and shrieking in his ears.

The Hill

* * *

Showered, changed, he was waiting for the city bus inside the main door of the school. It was dark outside and rain poured down. The halls were deserted.

"Why, hello, Phil," said a cheery voice behind him. He flinched and turned.

It was Miss Marzeau, in a red raincoat and carrying an umbrella. "Waiting for the bus?"

"Yes, ma'am."

"I'm headed home. You live on Dinant, don't you?"

"Near there. Redwood."

"Want a lift?"

"Oh, very much, thank you," Phil said politely.

Cheshire looked at him and thought again, *I can't believe what they say about this boy.* "It's in the lot to the right. Is that windbreaker waterproof? The door on your side'll be locked, so follow me out."

They ran through fat pelting drops of rain, through an ankle-deep puddle invisible in the dark, then they were in her car. It was a dark-red VW. Phil thought it was pretty cramped inside, but he didn't say so.

Cheshire pointed to his seat belt and he fumbled with the unfamiliar fastenings. The seats were close together and she had perfume or cologne on, different from Alex's. It was lighter, somehow more mature. It fitted her, he thought. He caught a profile of her sharp nose and prominent chin as she bent to start the little car.

She revved the engine and he was suddenly banged against the door as she sent the car lunging out of the lot and hauled it around the turn almost on two wheels. Water roared against the floorboards as she steered through a wide, deep puddle. "Washes the salt off," she yelled over the motor. He grabbed a handhold on the dash with his good hand and hung on.

The trip didn't take long. At each turn Marzeau appeared to wait 'til the last second before wrenching the wheel over violently. She braked before the turns and accelerated into them, like the racing drivers he'd read about. He was thrown forward against the belt as she braked hard in front of his house. The porch light was on. "Thanks, Miss Marzeau," he said. "You're a good driver."

"Why, thank you, Phil," she said warmly. He pulled at the handle, trying to open his door.

"Just a moment, before you leave."

"Ma'am?"

"Oh, that makes me feel so old. But never mind. I, well, just wanted to say that, though I don't know the details, I heard you're in some kind of trouble. At school. Now, Mr. Kroezler's the guidance counselor. He does know everything about college and scholarships. But just between the two of us, he's probably a bit hard to talk to for a young person with a problem. So . . . well, if you feel you need to talk things over with someone older, for advice, or just to get it off your chest, I live in the new building on Aspen Circle. I'll be glad to listen. And help any way I can."

"Why . . . thanks. Maybe . . . well, you're right," Phil said hesitantly. "I'm having problems, yeah. I don't think they're the kind anyone can help me with, but thanks for the offer."

"Okay." She smiled. "The handle farther back. Pull up."

"Oh, right. Well, g'night, Miss Marzeau. Thanks again." He got out and closed the door. It didn't sound like it had locked right. "Slam it, "she said. He slammed it, then ran home through the rain.

As he stood on the porch, taking off his wet things so as not to drip in the living room, he heard Jake and Mary arguing inside in high, strident voices.

TEN

When he opened the door the shouting stopped, and his parents looked shamefacedly at him and at each other.

"Hi, Mom. Jake, you're home early today," he said.

"Yeah," his stepdad said. "As a matter of fact, I've been home since noon. And I'll be here for ten more days."

"Say, that's great! We'll do some fishing this weekend, okay?"

His stepdad didn't answer. Mary said, "Phil, what he means is he's been given unpaid leave while the town board considers his punishment."

"Punishment? I thought he got chewed out already."

"That was Chief Bradner's decision, Phil," Jake said. "They didn't take his recommendation the way they normally do. They might even terminate me."

"For loaning me a car? Once?"

"Phil," Jacob said, sounding like he was fighting to stay patient, "In a small town like this, just like in a big city, there are interests. Two councilmembers are pressing this matter with the Department. Bill Brentano is Joe's grandfather. He owns two blocks of downtown. The other is Lionel V. Heckathorn. He works for Mr. Ryan.

"Frankly, Phil, I'm not sure how far the Chief can go to buck the council."

"Oh, God, Jake," Phil said. "I never thought they'd work like that. Try to mess with me through you."

"Well, when you have power, Phil, you use it. For some reason, probably to avoid scandal, they've decided not to prosecute you for assault or attempted rape. But the bottom line, I think, is, they want us out of town."

"But I didn't try to do that," Phil said. He couldn't get the word *rape* out of his mouth. Or his mind. "She's making that up. All I did was – "

"Yeah, yeah, I heard it, thanks. But look at it from their point of view. They're her parents and friends. They love her, like we love you. Since they weren't there, and you ran away before anyone else arrived, they believe her. Why would she make up a story? What motive would she have? None her parents know of. None I know of, either."

After a moment Mary said, "Now, we still believe you, Phil. But can you explain why she'd lie? It would help him a lot to be able to explain this."

Phil went to the closet and took out his long raincoat and hat. "I don't know why. Like, I really don't." He pulled his raincoat on. "I'm going out for a walk. I have to think about what to do."

"Wear your rubbers, Son," said Mary.

"Oh, Mom, lay off for a change," he snapped, and went out.

* * *

The rain was cold and fell heavily, slanted in its fall by a breeze from the east. The streetlights cast a feeble glow over the deserted streets and their light splashed on the puddles and mixed with the falling rain.

He turned to put the breeze at his back and began to walk

without much of a goal. After a while he came to the railroad tracks and turned onto them, walking on the ends of the ties whenever the bed was too rocky.

It was hard to get his head around how suddenly his world had turned from that of a fairly promising student, aspiring to become a doctor, to that of a sex maniac. A menace to the community. Last week he'd thought the upcoming cross-country season was the biggest challenge he had. Tomorrow, if Brentano had his way, he'd spend the season in hospital, or worse. He remembered hearing about a student killed in a knife fight in Petroleum City. It could happen.

And it all hinged on Ryan. He came back again to her lie. He'd always figured people acted according to their own perceptions, however mistaken, of what was right and true. But then, how could she be doing something so wrong, saying things that weren't true? Had his (admittedly) ill-advised attempt at intimacy offended her that much? Could she really have thought that hesitant caress was a rape attempt?

But maybe the fight, and Jake's suspension, were being arranged without her knowing.

It was possible, but he doubted it. She'd hear about it. Through her friends, even if Brentano and her parents kept her in the dark. If he'd overestimated her goodness, he didn't underestimate her intelligence service.

The tracks were leading past the newer part of town, which was dotted with a couple small shopping malls, apartment buildings, a park. He hopped off the tracks and headed for the park. It had a bandstand he could find cover at. The rain was leaking under the neck of the raincoat and he was shivering, soaked and chilly.

It's all, he reflected, *because I was fantasizing about her. It's really my own fault. If I'd just acted normal, just said good night . . .* She'd let him kiss her; turned her face and let him. It hadn't been that passionate. More of a peck. But that too might have come in time. . . .

No, he thought, cursing himself for the hundredth time for his stupidity. *I had to make a grab, like an animal.*

He walked on blindly through the rain, almost forgetting the cold in the whirlpool of self-reproach and loathing.

Passing headlights illuminated a street sign. Aspen Circle.

Now, there was an idea. Maybe Miss Marzeau could explain Alex's actions. She was always talking about motivation in the books they read. Teachers were supposed to have the answers, right? And she'd offered. Anyway, maybe he could get warm. He only realized when he thought this how cold he really was.

He entered the new-looking lobby and found her name on a mailbox. Cheshire. *That's a funny name. Like Lewis Carroll's cat. No wonder she doesn't mention it in class.* The mailbox said apartment F. After some hesitation, he climbed a flight of wide stairs.

Her door was solid-looking steel. It had a knocker and a tiny peephole. He raised the knocker, then changed his mind and rapped with his knuckles. After a moment he heard steps inside. Then a chain rattled and the heavy door swung wide.

She was in a long, soft-looking dressing gown. Her hair was down and her sharp, pale face was flushed. She held a fluted glass in one hand, and motioned him in with the other, smiling brightly. "Why, Mister Pirella. An unexpected pleasure.Please come in,I don't bite."

Overcoming his surprise at her appearance, he brushed past. *Well, what did I expect,* he thought. *She can't be dressed up all the time.*

Still, a casual Miss Marzeau seemed very different from her classroom self. Her apartment was small and rather bare, but neatly kept. His gaze lingered on a Chinese vase, a print, a bookcase. It looked like the home of somebody intelligent, self-disciplined, and lonely.

"Sit down, please," Cheshire said. Then, "Oh! You're soaked.

Here, give me your coat. What were you doing walking around in the rain?"

"Well, like you said, Miss Marzeau, come to you if I needed advice. I think maybe, um, I do." His teeth were chattering.

"*As* you said, Phil, not *like*. Well, I'm available tonight, fortunately. But you look so cold!"

"I guess I am, yeah."

"You go right in the bathroom and take those wet things off. I'll get a blanket and hand it in to you. And, if you want, a little splash of something might not do you any harm."

""Thanks." What he really needed was a hot bath and bed, but a blanket and a drink would probably work.

He squished into the bathroom, and took off his shoes, socks, trousers, and shirt. A thin hand reached through the just-cracked door with a fluffy blanket. He wrapped it around himself gratefully, wrung his clothes out into the tub, and hung them to dry. Rearranging the blanket for maximum warmth, he went back into the living room and sat down. Presently she came back in with a steaming mug. He sipped at it tentatively and after a few swallows began to feel deliciously warm both inside and out.

Cheshire settled down with her own glass. "Now, what was it you wanted to talk about?"

"Well, I'm in a lot of trouble, and I really don't understand why, or what I should do. You probably heard about it. I told my mom, and my step-dad, and they believed me. But they weren't too helpful. In fact, my step-dad's in trouble himself because of me. It all seems so unfair."

"Do you want to tell me just why you're in trouble, Phil?"

"Well, I guess it all started when Coach asked me if I wanted to run the Hill." She raised her eyebrows and he added, "Porcupine Hill. A nine-mile cross-country workout some kids run for practice."

"Nine miles? That seems awfully far."

"It's rough, all right. I can't do it yet without stopping to rest."

"Go on."

"Well, I ran it with Joe Brentano the first time. He's a super runner. Went to the state finals last year. Like I said, it was my first time, and I just couldn't make it, my leg gave out. Joe called me a quitter and a cripple. I took a swing at him, but I missed."

She sipped at her drink and studied him with an expression of intense concentration. It made him feel like she was really listening, trying to understand and help. He was beginning to feel very warm and a little lightheaded as well, probably from what he guessed was rum.

"The next day he spread this story I'd boasted about running it, then hot-dogged it during the run, and swung at him when he tried to get me to keep going."

"Hot dogged?"

"Oh, it means . . . kind of loafing along, not putting out."

"I see. Runners' slang."

"I guess. Anyway, he spread this story, and most of the guys believed it. They got down on me because Joe's such a hero. I mean, going to State and all."

She nodded encouragingly. "Okay."

"But Alex, Alex Ryan, she's in my class – "

"I know Alicia."

"Well, she acted friendly, when everybody else was down on me. I . . . always liked Alex, in fact I . . . used to daydream about her in class."

She laughed. "I've noted that faraway look. What exactly did you daydream about?"

He felt his face burning, and it wasn't just the alcohol. "Oh . . . you know. Just . . . sex, I guess."

She sat back and crossed her legs under the gown. "I see.

93

Well, let me tell you something, in confidence, okay? We all daydream about that. Even girls. It's all right, as long as you don't let it get out of hand."

"Well, anyway, I liked her, and she was so friendly I decided to ask her out.

"Hm." She rubbed her mouth with the back of her hand. "Had she been friendly like that before?"

"Not really. It was kind of a sudden thing, I guess."

"That might be significant. I mean, the timing. But go on. The date's when you got into trouble, I take it."

"Yeah, it was like . . . after the movie, we were at her house, alone, and I kissed her, and I thought she wanted me to . . . touch her."

He didn't explain and after a moment Cheshire had to probe. "Touch her. How?"

Um, on the chest. So I did, real gentle, but she screamed."

"She screamed?"

"Well, not right when I did it. She . . . called me names first."

Cheshire shook her head. "Phil, listen. I think I know what happened next. Was one of the names 'cripple'"?"

He closed his eyes. Nodded.

"And then you hit her, didn't you?"

"It was just a slap."

"And it was then she screamed."

He didn't answer, just looked away, at the Chinese vase in his teacher's warm little apartment. "Excuse me," she said after a little while. "Here, give me your mug."

Phil took advantage of her trip to the kitchen to rub his eyes with the soft corner of the red blanket.

She returned with both his mug and her glass refilled. "Here," she said, and sat beside him. "I heard the story she spread. It wasn't pretty. But do you understand why she told it that way?"

"No."

"Phil, she's proud. She thinks of herself as pretty far above the common herd. We teachers see that. In class, in the cafeteria, wherever she goes. She's pretty and her family's well off."

He listened intently.

"It sounds to me as if at first she wanted to use you to rile up Brentano. Since this occurred after your argument with him. Being nice to you would make him angry."

"Okay," he said.

"But then you made your attempt on her. Now, nothing wrong in that, Phil. Nothing for you to agonize about; that's the way it's done. If she'd really liked you, it might have been the start of something nice for both of you. Don't feel bad about that.

"But when you did it, she saw it as an insult, coming from someone she considered an inferior. It outraged her. You dared do it to her, Alex Ryan. It made her say the wrong thing to you. And in your case, Phil, there's one word that overwhelms your self-control.

"So, without thinking, you slapped her. I'm sure you were as surprised as she. And then, not unnaturally, she screamed."

"And then she had to explain why to her parents," he said.

"Which she did in the way best calculated to make herself look virtuous and you evil; and at the same time, made sure her original quarry is eager for your scalp."

"Oh," he said, slowly. "So she never really liked me."

Cheshire smiled sympathetically. "I'm afraid it looks that way to me." She put her hand on his shoulder. "I'm sorry your daydreams couldn't come true with her. But don't take it too hard. Someday they will, and it'll be lovely. I know it's a disappointment, Phil. We just have to keep living, and looking for the best in people, until we meet whoever we're meant for. You're young. You'll come out of this without much scar tissue."

"I'm not so sure," he said. "Emotionally, maybe. Physically, maybe not."

She frowned again. "What does that mean?"

"Remember what you said about Brentano being eager for my scalp? We're fighting tomorrow. With knives."

"Knives," Cheshire said.

"That's not the worst of it," he continued grimly. "They're using their influence to have my step-dad fired. He lent me his squad car for the date, and I banged it up getting away."

"They're crucifying you. How can they be so heartless?"

A flood of self-pity welled up at her gentle, worried tone. "I don't know," he groaned. He put his head down, into the folds of the blanket, and a dam broke before his long-suppressed tears.

She was so nice to him. He felt that here was a place, finally, where he could forget about what people thought about him and just cry without shame, like a little boy. He sobbed into the soft red blanket. After a moment he felt her arms around him, rocking him a little. "It'll be all right, Phil. Believe me, unlikely as it might seem right now, it will all turn out right."

* * *

She couldn't explain how or why it had happened. She'd liked him as a student. He was a promising pupil. And when he'd come to her apartment, as wet, cold, woebegone as a lost puppy . . . he'd needed a friend, someone who could see a little more clearly through the fog that surrounded him.

But somehow her own need or hunger had taken over, and now, lying beside him in her neat little bedroom with a nosegay of violets on the bedside table, it had led her into something she couldn't quite believe she'd actually done, either as a teacher or as a woman.

Maybe he'd needed it, the consolation, though he could have done without it. But maybe it was more that it was what she herself had needed on this particular night.

Not for him, she thought, staring up at the ceiling in the near-darkness as Wolfe turned restlessly at their feet. *Just my own selfishness? Okay, maybe.* But despite her self-reproaches, a warm core of satisfaction glowed deep down inside. She didn't feel guilty. Not yet, at least.

Phil lay beside her, naked, face down, his good right arm still extended possessively across her waist. He was awake too, though he was still because he thought Cheshire was asleep and didn't want to wake her. He was drowsy and warm and exhausted, but a small stream of thought still trickled through his floating mind. *My first time*, he thought sleepily. Miss Marzeau — probably he should call her Cheshire now — had helped him. Showed him what to do. He'd never really been able to picture what it would be like, the warmth, the sense of complete intimacy, the dissolution and frenzy when he'd felt all-powerful and at the same time infinitely vulnerable. It was different from the hurried classes in Family Living, the line diagrams in the books, the coarseness of the locker-room jokes and stories. Just so different from everything else in his life, the busy, greedy, mean people, the endless shabbiness and mediocrity and worry about money.

She stirred, interrupting his thoughts. He shifted his arm, unwilling to cumber her. She sat up and he blinked again at her small pink pointed breasts in the dim light from the living room. She leaned in on one arm and kissed him again, on the mouth, so caressingly he felt himself stir again.

"You'd better be going," she said softly. "It's nearly midnight. Your dad and mom'll be wondering where you've got to in this downpour."

He stroked her back, still unable to believe, unable to keep his hands from exploring this new universe, discovered for the first time. She caught his hand, pressed it against her breast for a moment. "That's enough, now," she said. "You should be going, really."

He rolled out and began to search the floor for his clothing, and was startled and embarrassed when she switched on the light to help. Cheshire smiled at his efforts to cover himself. *He has a nice body,* she thought. Slim but with well-defined muscle. Only the arm, bent and shriveled like a chicken's wing, marred the symmetry. She realized suddenly that his instinctive effort when the light came on had been to cover not his privates, but that arm, and that even now he had it turned away from her as he dressed. She looked away and drew on her nightgown. She went into the bathroom and closed the door.

Phil finished dressing. Now what? He spotted his mug on the nightstand and finished it at a pull.

The bathroom door opened and Cheshire came out. "Need to use it? Before you go?"

"Yes, thank you," he said, and felt silly at speaking so formally. He urinated, and as the stream waned he wondered whether he should wash himself, like he'd read in one of Jacob's magazines. *I didn't use a rubber, either. Will I get something? God, I hope not. And what about her? What if . . . .*

He washed his hands and pulled on his still-damp shirt and trousers.

When he came out again she was waiting in the living room. She held out his raincoat. "Almost dry," she said without looking at him. "And I think it's letting up."

She helped him with the sleeve without him having to ask.

"Cheshire," he said, and it didn't sound as strange as it had on her mailbox. "Will you be all right? I mean . . . we didn't use. . . ."

"Don't worry. But you're a dear for thinking of it."

He turned to leave but halted. He had to ask one more question. "Um . . . are you sorry? About what we did?"

She smiled in a strange way, a faraway smile. But kissed him lightly on the lips. "You know, to be totally honest, I'm not really sure just yet. But right now, go." And opening the door, she ushered him out with a firm hand to his lower back.

ELEVEN

When his alarm went off he struggled up into consciousness and reached out and shut it off. Five-thirty. It would go off again in ten minutes.

Ten minutes later he was reawakened from the same delicious dream about Cheshire and decided to get up. Despite only five hours' sleep he felt great.

Then he remembered today was the day he'd face Joe Brentano with a knife in his hand.

He tramped slowly downstairs and forced himself to eat a few slices of toast and marmalade and drink some orange juice. Presently he found himself thinking about Cheshire again.

She was different from the girls at school. She listened. She understood. *And,* he thought, *once you stop thinking of her as your teacher, she's really hot.*

By the time he finished breakfast, washed his dishes, and put them away, he was in love.

He felt better about the fight as he started to walk to school. A walk was a good compromise between running, which would waste energy he might need that afternoon, and riding the bus. *If she loves me, everything will be all right. Somehow.*

Inside his trousers, the five-inch hunting blade, filched from Jake's hunting gear, bumped hard and sharp against his thigh with each step. He'd wrapped it in a brown paper sandwich bag.

He reached school ahead of the bus, since he'd started so early. He went swinging through the corridors, humming. No one spoke to him today, either, but it didn't seem to matter as much. He opened his locker, slid the knife inside quickly, and decided to write Cheshire a note.

He took out a pad of lined paper, clicked his pen, and wrote:

> *Dear Cheshire,*
> *I've been thinking about you since last night. Being with you and*

(here he hesitated, then wrote firmly)

> *making love to you was the best thing that's ever happened to me. I hope you are not sorry, and that we can see each other again. Whatever happens today, remember me.*
> *Love,*
> *PHIL.*

He reread it and smiled. Dignified yet intimate. Most of all, he wanted her to know he cared, it wasn't just a one-night stand.

Maybe I'm not so dumb with girls after all, he thought smugly.

He folded the sheet 'til it was small and tucked it inside the cover of his English notebook. The bell rang for first period. But as he turned to go, cutting suddenly into his pleasure slashed a fearfully real image of a gleaming, razor-edged switchblade.

* * *

Cheshire too was at school early that morning. She sat at her desk and busied herself averaging grades while her home-room students eddied in and out.

The situation was impossible. How had it happened? Or rather, how had she allowed it to happen, since she was older and in a position of responsibility. She hadn't slept all night worrying, and had reached no conclusion, except that staying up made her eyes puffy. The rum? Neither of them had been too drunk to know what was happening. And alcohol only weakened inhibitions, it didn't create desire that wasn't there.

She had to decide what to do. Pirella could probably be relied on to keep quiet, if she asked him to, and if he didn't feel he had to brag about it, which she doubted he would. And even if he did, she could deny it. Although she hated to think about it that way, who would believe his word against hers?

Even thinking that made her ashamed. *I condemn others for lying about him, but I'd do the same thing if it would benefit me? I'm just as big a hypocrite as anybody else,* she thought. Anyway, she could contain it. It'd be awkward with him in class, but it would only be for another six or seven months. And he was a good student, he'd be leaving town after graduation for college or a job somewhere else.

The important thing was that it didn't happen again. She had to end it now, for good. Not see him again. Outside of school, o course. She'd ask him to stay after class today and tell him. She just hoped he'd be reasonable and not start saying he loved her.

She frowned to herself. But what if he did? No man ever had before . . . no, that was stupid. She had to cut it off, now, before it went any further.

Then she remembered today was the day of his fight.

* * *

When AP English began Phil was in his accustomed seat. But he didn't so much as glance at Alex Ryan, who looked drawn and exhausted. He had eyes only for Miss Marzeau.

But she didn't look or meet his gaze. She acted withdrawn. Less enthusiastic about her pet authors. The class caught the mood and grew restless. Some of the rowdier students in the rear began to fight, and she sent them out into the hall. After that things quieted down again, but the class was still uneasy, on edge.

Fifty minutes is too long this morning, she thought. *For them, and for me.*

* * *

When the bell rang at last he dawdled at his desk, rearranging his books. No one spoke to him as the rest of the class filed and pushed their way out. When they were alone he went up to where she sat, her eyes downcast, and handed her the note. "Miss Marzeau," he said, the formal name sounding strange now, "I won't see you again before this afternoon. I want you to keep this in case something happens."

"Phil, you can't fight with knives. Neither of you understands how serious this is. You could be maimed, or even killed. It's too dangerous. Don't do it. Please."

He couldn't answer. How could he explain? This wasn't a machismo thing. This was the first time in his whole life anyone had offered to fight him as an equal. If he turned this down because he was afraid of being hurt — and God knew he was familiar with pain, a lot better than she was — he'd never feel whole. Finally he said, "I'm sorry, it's just something I really have to do. Here."

She slowly extended her hand and took the tightly-folded paper. *A high-school love note,* she thought numbly. *I can't stop this fight. They'll hold it somewhere we won't see it.*

He touched her thin hand. "So long," he said, and swallowed. Yes, he'd say it. "Um, I love you," he muttered, and turned and walked out.

She felt her eyes fill as he left. She couldn't help it. Like

Sidney Carton at the end of *A Tale of Two Cities*. But after a moment she dried her eyes and blew her nose.

I've got to stop this, she thought. And there was only one foolproof way to do it.

* * *

Phil sat transfixed in his seat all through last period. He felt weird, detached, as if he were floating somewhere behind his seated body and only using its eyes as remote television monitors. Only his bowels kept him in contact with reality, though there was really nothing left to evacuate.

At the last bell he pushed his way out with the rest, heedless of angry looks. A few kids, though, stepped aside and made way for him. He wondered if they'd heard. Hell, he thought, knowing Brentano, he'd probably invited an audience.

He threw his books into his locker without sorting them and pulled out the sandwich bag. He hefted it, then stuck the parcel into his rear pocket. It stuck out, but with the wrapping no one could guess what it was unless they already knew where he was headed.

He pushed open the door to the parking lot. A knot of boys was waiting. They were silent, but as he walked through he felt a pat on the back. *So*, he thought, *not everybody's against me.* The thought didn't cheer him much.

A figure to the left caught his eye. The lanky stride, the tall silhouette . . . Brentano, emerging from the locker room. A few of their teammates trailed him. Carl Saarlo saw Phil and gave him a furtive thumbs-up. He tried to smile back, but managed only a weak grimace.

A familiar tinny roar caught his ear, and an instant later a red blur shot out of the teachers' parking. Brentano didn't see it until the last second. He hesitated, then turned to run back toward the school, but too late. A terrifying shriek of rubber drew every eye as the little car, rear wheels locked by panicky braking, fishtailed viciously and smashed broadside into the senior.

Phil was one of the first to get to it. Cheshire was at the wheel, shaking hands over her bowed face, sobbing and screaming inside the stalled Volkswagen.

* * *

The ambulance and the police had come and gone, and the rest of the team had gone home. Cheshire had been in no condition to drive and had left in a squad car.

Phil was finally alone in the deserted lot. He walked about at random for a while, then went down to the locker rooms.

Coach Anderson was sitting on a folding chair, holding two pair of new fifteen-ounce gloves. "Pirella. You ready? Where's Joe?"

"Coach, there's been an accident. He was hit by a car."

"Oh, no." Anderson slowly hung the gloves on a nearby peg. "Is he hurt bad?"

"I think so. He was out when the EMTs came, so they took him to the hospital in Hodges."

"That's a good half-hour trip. God, we need a hospital in this town."

"No lie, Coach," Phil said. He left Anderson and went to his locker to dress out.

* * *

He jogged along the straight near the top of the first hill. The reserve of energy his body had been building up all day had propelled him to this point almost effortlessly. His legs felt strong. His lungs weren't so great, but they'd hold out, he hoped.

He turned right onto the rise and ran up it very slowly.

Then he was over, and headed down into the valley.

It was quiet today. Almost no wind, and the few clouds in the late afternoon sky hung stationary above the hilltops. The trees, too, were silent. He let his legs move naturally, rhythmically, let gravity take over, and like a gliding hawk drifted down into the valley. His mind rested too. He didn't want to think just now.

At the bottom he put a little more effort into his pace. The road levelled out and widened to become a dusty asphalt line between silent fields. The dogs were· quiet today, and stayed out of sight. The loudest sound was the scuff-scuff of his running shoes on the shoulder and the harsher rasp of his breathing.

He'd gone to one breath per stride over the hill, and now he felt lightheaded. He went back to the three-count rhythm, keying it to the fall of his left foot. He ran fairly slowly and the still landscape flowed steadily by.

Gradually some deeper level of his brain took charge of the business of running. He replayed Brentano's expression as the side of the skidding car traveled the last few feet before it hit him. The impact had torn a small black object from somewhere about his body. It had slid, twirling on the pavement, to vanish underneath an old Chevy.

Phil had retrieved the switchblade while everyone else had clustered about the motionless body. He paused now for a moment at the bridge, looked both ways, then chucked it into the rocky stream.

He saw Cheshire's face, horrified at what she'd done, hiding herself with both hands. He'd been unable to touch or comfort her, or thank her. There'd been too many others around, and so she was alone, until the police had arrived to ask their questions.

Would Brentano live? He hoped so. She'd struck him with the rear quarter of her car, a smooth surface without projections, and he'd bounced off rather than been knocked across the lot or run over. She hadn't been going that fast. Really, she'd handled it really well. Joe had been hurt, but he'd likely live.

Would he run again? That wasn't as easy to answer. A serious injury hardly ever completely healed. The doctors could try, but a champion's body was so finely honed any scar tissue, any weakly knit bone or untrustworthy ligament, would relegate him to the ranks of the also-rans.

Could Brentano live as an also-ran? In spite of his braggadocio, his bullying manner, had he not conquered the Hill? Was he not a State champion? Running, maybe more than any other sport, depended on willingness to withstand pain.

But to maintain that willingness in the face of certain failure . . . that was something else again. The answer could only come from deep within a runner's soul.

He began to climb the upgrade leading to the switchbacks that would carry him up the first portion of Porcupine.

And what would happen to Cheshire? Her abrupt, reckless style of driving must have been observed by others around town. But would they know this seeming recklessness was tempered with the skill Cheshire had showed him?

When they left school, the students normally kept to the sidewalks ringing the lot. Only later, when the teachers had left, did the runners leave by the locker room door to cross the lot to the track or the football field. Brentano, coming out so early, was breaking routine, and in an area Cheshire could have expected to be free of pedestrians just then. He hoped she'd thought of that in her defense.

He reached the first switchback and turned. The grade became steeper, then still steeper. His wind was getting short and his legs were laboring. No cramps, though. His jaw started to ache. That wasted energy. He relaxed it, checked his neck and shoulders for tension, relaxed them, too and ran on. His mouth and throat were painfully dry but he couldn't stop breathing to swallow.

And what about Alex? She'd been pushed to the back of his mind, but now he wondered about her again. With Cheshire in his corner he could stand the silencing. In time, if he showed it wasn't that big a deal to him, some of his friends at least would let it go. And now, thanks to Cheshire, he could understand why Alex had done it, a little. That made it easier, too.

But one problem remained: How to save Jake from paying for his stepson's too-hasty temper, his uncontrolled sensitivity to a word or tone of scorn.

If the fight had occurred, and he, Phil, had been badly hurt, maybe they'd have called the dogs off Jake. But that wouldn't work now. He could leave town for school somewhere else, but that would take money for travel and board, money his family didn't have.

He could drop out. Find a job in some other town. If he left there'd be no reason for them to fire Jake. Jake was a good cop. He'd been commended twice.

But if I drop out I'll never be a doctor.

He turned left onto the last switchback before the last stretch of road. It wound clockwise halfway around Porcupine, and was very steep indeed. The switchback was no picnic either. His calves gave a warning tremor. Red pains from his throat and lungs shot through his head. Slowing even more, he began climbing sidewise, pacing up the hill like a crab, zig-zagging from side to side.

At the end of the switchback he started up the final rise. It was like trying to run up a ladder. After twenty yards his abused body came to a standstill, running very slowly in place, but not able to move another step upward. He stopped.

He was walking around in a little circle, taking deep, slow breaths, when his mouth filled suddenly with saliva. A second later he was vomiting by the side of the road. There wasn't much to come up, but the dry heaves were worse. He looked up, wiping his mouth with the back of his hand. Another quarter of a mile, four hundred yards, would have seen him to the top.

* * *

"Run Team Run Team Run Team RUN!
"Raymondsville – FIGHT!'"
Sheila Conrad brought her pompom down hard, all the way to her feet, then exploded upward in a spring that took her feet three feet off the floor and sent her chestnut hair flying. She landed and held the pose, arms outstretched for a moment, smiling brilliantly at an imagined audience; then relaxed. "Let's call it a day, girls," she said gaily. "Same time tomorrow. This will be the peppiest cross-country meet Raymondsville 's ever seen."

The other cheerleaders scattered, muttering about the hours Conrad forced them to practice. Sheila pretended not to hear. They'd elected her as the varsity cheer captain, and there was no honor in leading a second-rate squad. Besides, the exercise was good for their figures. Two of the freshmen could definitely stand to shed some poundage.

She slipped the pompoms off her wrists and strolled languidly through the darkened, empty corridors. Her footsteps echoed off the tiled walls and the gray metal doors of lockers.

Noticing a small wad of paper on the floor, she picked it up. It was lined paper, tightly folded, obviously dropped by accident just outside Miss Marzeau's classroom.

Sheila stopped dead. Her eyes grew wide as she read and reread it. She gasped aloud, and read it a third time with growing excitement. Then squealed, and bounced on her toes, clapping. Could it be real? It was like a movie, or the 'domestic dramas' her mom liked to watch on daytime TV. 'Cheshire' and 'Phil' . . .

making love? No, it couldn't be. It was a joke.

But then she stiffened as a new thought occurred. The accident in the parking lot, as all the girls knew, had prevented a fight between Pirella and Joe.

Could this note link an apparent coincidence to something deeper? Something . . . guiltier?

She refolded the note and thrust it into her sweater pocket. Then hesitated in the empty corridor.

She could return it. To Marzeau, or to Pirella. No, not *him*, she didn't want to be seen with *that* creep. Or, she could pass it on to someone who'd be interested . . . say, the police, or the principal, or . . . better than either, to Alex. She'd know how to use it, and her parents had connections where it counted.

Yes, I'll give it to Alex, she thought. Then went to her tiptoes and pirouetted.

But how does that do me any good?

She'd have to make her promise that Sheila would be mentioned, that Shelia Conrad had uncovered the truth. Ryan had a bad habit of appropriating the glory when a sweet piece of news came along. That couldn't happen this time! A teacher and a student. Why, this was the biggest thing that had happened so far this year! Pirella and Marzeau! She chuckled and hugged herself. *I liked Miss Marzeau, but this is too big for a coverup. If she was innocent, she could just deny it. Say Pirella made it up, that was all.*

But what if she *admitted* it? Dow delicious that would be!

She burst into a run, footsteps echoing in the empty corridor.

* * *

No, Alex thought, reading the note again, then hungrily starting over. It couldn't be . . . but it did seem to make sense out of the 'accident' that afternoon. She lifted her eyes to meet

Sheila's eager brown ones. "Where'd you find this, Sheila?"

"In the hall, outside Marzeau's room. She must've dropped it on her way out to run Joe over."

"I wonder how long this has been going on. I've never seen anything between them in class."

"Look here, where it says 'since last night'. It sounds to me as if it just started then."

Alex read the note through a third time, then refolded it. "This is dynamite," she said soberly. "It's more than something to gossip about. This'll get her fired. Or even put in jail."

"Only if it's true. And if it is, she deserves what she gets. Teachers aren't supposed to play around with the students."

"I suppose you're right. So, we get this to the principal. And a few other people might be interested, too."

"But we can tell the girls about it, can't we?"

"Why, dear Sheila, I wouldn't dream of interfering with your freedom of speech." Alex smiled. "But you'll have to be fast if you want it to be news. Right after dinner, my phone's going to be red hot."

TWELVE

Arriving on the scene, the police had confirmed the boy wasn't in immediate danger. Sergeant Julius Hoffnagel, one of the two officers nearby when the dispatcher called, checked the injured party's pulse and respiration. Both were strong. There was no evidence of compound fracture and only slight bleeding from superficial injuries. But the boy was unconscious.

"Don't move him," Hoffnagel told his partner. "Get on the radio, check on the EMTs." He turned his attention to the sobbing woman in the car. He opened her door. "Ma'am? Would you mind coming over and sitting with me for a little while? We need to ask you some questions."

Cheshire didn't remember the note again till she got home that night. The police had taken a long time with questions, but had, she felt, finally been convinced by her distraction and very real horror that Brentano had just been in the wrong place at the wrong time. *Although,* she thought, mixing a dark and stormy in her little kitchen, *they left the impression my driving habits could be more sedate.*

Of course, she was legally at fault, since she'd failed to stop for a pedestrian. He had the right of way wherever he was. But they hadn't given her a breathalyzer or a walk test, and had even given her a ride home.

She sat down on her sofa and gulped the drink. *I did it,* she thought, with mixed revulsion and triumph. *He's hurt, yes, but I heard the officer on the radio: no fracture, no major blood loss. He won't die, and there won't be a fight. So I might have saved Joe, too.*

"I'd better destroy that note," she said to Wolfe, who was interested in her drink. "No, you don't like those, remember?"

It wasn't in her purse, where she thought she'd put it. Nor in her briefcase with her papers. *I must have left it in my desk drawer. I was too upset to remember exactly what I did with it. I'll burn it tomorrow morning.*

* * *

But when she sat down at her desk the next day, the note she found was on top of, and not in, her desk; and though addressed to her, wasn't from Phil but from Reba, the school secretary. Mr. Ashberne, the principal, wanted to see her in his office as soon as she got in. One of the student teachers would be in to take her classes.

She sat holding the note for a few minutes, fighting a sinking sensation. Then took her key ring from her purse and unlocked her desk. There was no small, folded-up note.

The first few of her home-room students filed blithely in. Finally she opened her briefcase, centered the day's lesson plans on her desk, and scribbled down a homework reading. She re-locked her desk and went out into the hall. She walked to the main office, greeting people along the way, and half-opened the door. "I got your note, Reba. Thanks ever so much. Is he in yet?"

"He came in early today. I think he's waiting to see you. Why don't you go right in?"

When she opened the frosted door Ashberne glanced up

from his screen, then leaned his body back in the revolving chair. It gave an authoritative squeak. He folded his fingers and studied her over them. Graying temples added the last touch to his carefully curated image of the kindly but efficient administrator. "Please sit down, Miss Marzeau. We have some serious issues to discuss."

She sank into the low stuffed chair to the right of his desk. Ashberne looked down at her over his fingertips and smiled. *This chair does half his work for him,* she thought fleetingly.

"Well, to business." He reached into a pocket and flipped a small object on the polished wood between them. Cheshire had to sit up in her chair before she could see what it was.

"Have you ever seen this before?"

"Yes," she said levelly.

"It's addressed to you, from a student in your class named . . . " He glanced at a note on his blotter.

"Philip Pirella."

"Ah, yes, Pirella. Quite. Ahem."

"That is a private communication, Mr. Ashberne. May I have it back, please?"

"No. It was found on school property. During school hours. Why, in your opinion, did he write this . . . mash note?"

Mash note, she thought. *Now that's dated.* Aloud she said, "I presume because he thinks he's in love with me, Mr. Ashberne." She disliked this self-important man and his prissy manner.

"Yes. I agree. Quite evident from the, ah, phrasing of the missive." She said nothing and a long pause ensued. Ashberne became increasingly fidgety, and Cheshire began to lose her own fear as she watched him squirm behind the massive desk.

"What I meant to say, Miss Marzeau – or rather, what I, ah, meant to ask, was. . . . "

"Whether we actually 'made love', as he puts it."

"Exactly," said Ashberne, with a chuckle. "Of course, I know

114

how a boy's imagination can sort of – "

"Yes, Mr. Ashberne, I'm afraid we did."

His mouth made a droll round O of shock. "Good grief . . . Are you serious? Do you realize what you're saying?"

"I do. I won't say I'm proud of it, because I'm not. For someone in my position, it was inexcusable. For a woman . . . maybe that's a different matter."

Ashberne rose suddenly from his chair and began pacing back and forth, hands behind his back. Then he stopped short and pointed a dramatic finger. "You're a disgrace to the teaching profession."

She laughed a little, drily. "I know."

The principal's expression suddenly changed, grew cunning. He bent over his desk toward her, looking like an effeminate weasel as he smiled. "I'm sorry I said that, Cheshire. Of course he did it against your will. I've heard about this particular *lad* before. He's the one who attacked the Ryan girl, isn't he?"

She half-rose from her low chair. "No!" she said in a voice that made Reba, outside, stop typing and look at the frosted door. Then, more calmly, "He never attacked anyone. Alicia made that story up. All he did was kiss her. As for me, it was my fault. If it was a fault."

Ashberne, looking harried, patted the air. "Now, now, no need to get upset. Surely we can discuss this in a rational manner, as adults. Please sit down."

She sat down again and the principal fussed about for a moment, retrieved the note, tucked it away, and sat once more. The chair squeaked threateningly. "If this is true, the Board will expect your resignation. Effective immediately. Reba will give you the format."

"They won't get it," she said. "I had outstanding grades at Teacher's College. The Board was overjoyed when I accepted their invitation to teach here, considering the ridiculous salary.

This is one small indiscretion, and I daresay most of the teachers here have some such skeleton tucked away. Don't you?"

Ashberne colored. "My character is not at discussion here."

"Under discussion, Mr. Ashberne. Not at. You should read Fowler on Idiom. You're starting to confuse yours."

He rose with offended dignity. "The question of your retention or dismissal is, fortunately for us both, beyond my purview. The School Board will be duly informed of this matter. You will have the opportunity of presenting your case before decision is rendered. I personally can't condone your behavior, but I'll admit that I have been, thus far at least, satisfied with your work and teaching ability. I will, if you desire, state that in your defense. And wish you the best of luck."

Cheshire rose too. "I'd appreciate that very much. I value your good opinion. And I'm sorry this matter has come between us."

Ashberne inclined his head. Taking it as dismissal, she left and walked back toward her classroom. Relieved for at least one thing: Ashberne hadn't made any connection between the note and Brentano's accident. Yet, at least.

Then she stopped short in the corridor and closed her eyes.

The engine roared and she floored the pedal a few times to make sure it wouldn't falter when she gunned it. She closed her eyes and inhaled to steady her fingers, which were trembling on the wheel. Don't let me hurt him, she prayed. Just enough to stop it.

She opened her eyes and fixed her attention on what she had to do.

Brentano would have to walk twenty yards up a sidewalk from the locker room door before he was hidden from view by the chain-link fence surrounding the lot. She looked at her watch again. 3:05.

The moment he appeared she tramped on the accelerator. The seat belt squeezed her thundering heart as she rounded the corner and exited the teachers' lot. There he was, stepping off the curb.

Then the terrible scream of her locked tires, the awful crunching bang as

116

a human body stopped the swinging weight of metal. . . .

Standing in the hall, she began to shake again, the way she had as the police were asking their interminable questions. She hadn't had to pretend to be shocked. She'd been near collapse, and the cop had been gentle with her. *I did it to save them both, not hurt them. Maybe I could have done it a better way, but there wasn't time. Hadn't been time to think of one. Only time to act, so I acted.*

What would she say in front of the board? There was a PTA meeting that night. But it might be best if she didn't go.

The students walking around her in the hall were looking at her strangely. She took a grip and went on toward the lot. She wondered absently how the sub was doing with first period.

* * *

Phil hadn't planned to go to school Friday morning. Instead, when he got up, he dressed in loose old jeans arid a sweatshirt, both clean, but not up to the dress code.

At six-thirty, when he knew she'd be in, he phoned Reba at the main office and told her some story or other he hoped she wouldn't call his parents to check out. What he really intended that morning was to go see Brentano at the hospital.

I'll need all day for that, to Hodges and back, he thought, finishing a bowl of Cheerios. He'd wear his jogging shoes. That'd be a change from the Hill workout, and he could use a change. It was fifteen miles away. About three hours if he alternated running and walking, and if they saw him on the road, somebody might give him a ride. He washed the bowl and put it away, changed his shoes, and was out of the house before Jake or Mary came downstairs.

It was cold, making him glad he'd dressed warmly, but the sky was cloudless; it would be warm later. The sun was just clear of the hills that surrounded Raymondsville and already too

117

brilliant to look at directly. He jogged along at an easy pace, eager to get out of town, but conscious he had a long way to go.

It took him a little over two hours to get to Hodges. The road between the towns was level and fairly wide, winding between hills and only occasionally climbing gently to negotiate a saddle. For most of the way the road followed a creek, sometimes crossing it on concrete bridges dating from the projects of the 'thirties. The valley was largely wooded, but from time to time he passed abandoned farm buildings or old gas stations, long innocent of paint or window-glass, surrounded by fields overgrown by weeds and wild blackberry canes.

Toward nine o'clock a battered-looking old man in a manure-stained Dodge pickup gave him a lift for about three miles, before he had to turn off to 'see a feller about some sick cows.' Phil had the feeling he'd met the old guy somewhere before, but couldn't place him.

He walked the last mile into Hodges. It was warm now and he was tired. He asked a mailman for directions to the hospital.

When he checked at Reception the woman on duty was unwilling to let him go up. "But I'm his brother," he lied. She eyed his sweat-stained clothing, but gave him directions to a room on the fifth floor. On the way to the elevator he saw a fountain and filled his gut with cold water. Bad practice for a runner, but he was too thirsty to care. *Besides, I'll be able to rest for a while before I have to start back*, he thought as the elevator arrived.

The door to Number 514 was open and he went in, his jogging shoes silent on the tiled floor.

Brentano was lying in bed with his eyes closed. He was swathed with bandages and plaster about the face, looking like a Smokey Stover battered husband. The rest of his body was covered with a blanket. One leg was raised in traction. Phil sat down next to the bed and Brentano opened his eyes at the creak.

"Hi, Joe." Phil forced an uncertain smile.

Brentano closed his eyes as if in disgust and said nothing; then apparently thought better of it and opened them again. "Pirella," he whispered. "Ready to kill or be killed, man?"

"I consider it postponed, Joe. No reason we can't be friends 'til then, though. I'm sorry you got hurt."

"Yeah. Me too."

"Are you in a lot of pain?"

"Nah." He closed his eyes again. "Actually, it's funny, I can't feel a thing. Doesn't hurt a bit, except for these cuts on my face."

A chill touched the back of Phil's neck. "You can't feel a thing?" he repeated stupidly, then immediately wished he hadn't.

"Can't move my arms or legs. They say I have to lie here for a few days before they can take a scan. They fixed my leg, though."

"Christ," said Phil. "That doesn't sound too good, Joe."

"No, it don't to me either." Brentano was silent a moment, then roused himself with an effort. He opened his eyes again but the lids began drooping again almost at once. "They got me all doped up so I don't worry about things. I might drop off on you here."

"That's okay, buds. I hope you get better quick."

"I don't think I'll be running much anymore, crip. Oh, sorry. Sorry, Phil. I didn't mean that. Say, you used to be pretty much like this, didn't you? When you were little?"

"Kind of. Yeah. I was in a wheelchair for a long time, and my one arm was too far gone to save. But listen, if you've got balls, they can't keep you in a bed. You're a champ, Joe. No matter what, you'll run again. I'll help if you want."

"Thanks. You know . . . you're the only one's come out to see me except my family. Alex didn't . . . say, I think I'm gonna zonk out for a little while here. Don't go away."

"I won't, Joe," said Phil. He stayed until an officious nurse made him leave.

* * *

"Sir, Mr. Ashberne, on line two." said Augustin Ryan's secretary over his intercom.

"Thanks," said Ryan. He picked up. "Ashberne. This is Augustin Ryan. Have you heard about this sex scandal my daughter's been telling me about?"

"Oh., yes indeed., Counselor," said Ashberne quickly. "I've just been speaking with the teacher in question."

"Well?"

"Well, sir, she – ah – admits it's true, but she doesn't intend to resign. She refuses to lay the blame on the boy."

"What?"

"She says it's true, but she won't – "

"I heard you the first time. What I want to know is, are you going to let this kind of behavior go unpunished?"

"Well, Mr. Ryan, I'm only the principal. I mean, I can't terminate a teacher's contract. Only the Board can do that. And they have to give her a hearing."

"Who's on the board, again?"

"Why, Mr. Barnholdt, Chief Bradner, Mrs. Smith from the PTA; Mr. Agerholm, Mrs. Sangner, and the elder Mr. Brentano. Plus two or three others that don't really count."

Ryan noted the names on a memo pad. "Thanks. Say, we can depend on you to defend the good name of the community, can't we?"

"Why, indeed yes, Counselor. In every respect. That goes without saying."

"Good," said Ryan. He hung up, then pressed the button on his intercom. "Rita, get me Ed Barnholdt. Call him at his office."

THIRTEEN

Phil got back from Hodges around four. He'd been held up by an afternoon shower, from which he'd sheltered in a school-bus shed. He was too tired to do anything but trudge the last few miles, and his clothes were wet and dirty when he let himself in at home.

His parents, seated in the living room, looked up as he came in but said nothing. He went up to his bedroom and started to change. *I think I'll take a shower before dinner, too*, he thought.

The phone rang downstairs as he struggled out of his damp trousers. "Phil, it's for you," his mother called. He pulled on a dry pair and went downstairs to take it.

"Phil?"

"Yeah. Who's this?"

"This is Miss . . . this is Cheshire."

"Oh. Hi," he said, suddenly happy.

"Something's come up. We need to talk. Can you come to my apartment tonight?"

"Sure. When?"

"Anytime. After dinner."

"Okay. I'll be there about seven."

"Fine," she said. They both hesitated.

"Well, good-bye." She hung up.

Phil replaced the handset, thought for a moment, then went back upstairs to finish changing.

Mary had made a casserole. It looked and smelled delicious when she lifted the lid. "Tuna noodle," Jake said, bending to inhale the fragrant steam. "I could eat this all week."

"If I made this as often as you'd eat it you wouldn't fit into that uniform. You're starting to hang over your gun belt as it is."

"How's the review going, Dad? Heard anything?" Phil asked.

"No, and it's strange," Jake said, dipping copious helpings onto each plate in turn, saving his own for last. "I've been trying to keep tabs by having lunch with the guys, but not a word can they tell me."

"You'd think they would have decided something by now," said Mary anxiously. "Phil, have some broccoli. It's good for you, it'll help your running."

"Yeah, you'd think so . . . maybe that means they've decided ·to keep me after all. If they do, that means that you, young man, have got to lie low and stay out of any more trouble. Understand me? Just watch your step. Be a goody-goody for a while."

He winced, but said, "I'll sure try, Dad." *Cheshire and me are going to have to be super careful*, he thought. If that ever got loose . . . more trouble wouldn't help with the department. He was sorry to have gotten Jake in trouble, but all he could do now was keep his head down and his nose clean.

"What are you doing tonight, Phil?" his mom said brightly.

"Um, I'll be going out after supper."

"Another date?"

"No. Not really. Just out."

"You know, Phil," Mary said, "You haven't been spending as much time as you used to on your studies. I think you're too tired. You run too much. Why, sometimes you come in after school and you're limping like you can hardly walk."

"You have to run a lot when you're on the cross-country

team, Mom."

"I know that! I'm not stupid, even if I am just your mother. I can see what you're doing to yourself. I only want what's best for you."

"I know. I'll try to study harder," he said, trying not to lose his temper. His mother always treated him like a little boy. A crippled, helpless little boy. What would it take before she realized he'd grown up?

"Well, that's better," she said. They ate in silence for a few minutes. Until she added, "But you'd better not go out tonight."

"Dammit, Mom," he cried, his overstrained temper carrying him away, "Why can't you leave me alone. Stop telling me what to do. I'm not a kid anymore!" He threw down his fork so violently it bounced past his startled parents onto the floor. He got up from the table and started to go upstairs., then changed his mind and blindly stormed out.

"Phil!" his stepdad called after him as the front door closed, but he didn't want to hear it.

"Now, what set him off like that?" Mary asked Jake. "He's gotten so unreasonable. I'm just trying to give him some good advice, but he just won't listen."

Jake looked at her, then went back to his tuna and noodles.

* * *

As he walked down Redwood his temper cooled and his trembling stopped. *Jesus,* he thought, *I really lost control in there.* The sudden violence of his temper in the last year or so scared him sometimes. Granted, he was under pressure, but where would Jake be as a cop if he lost his shit when a speeder gave him lip? But when he got angry all the frustration and uncertainty seemed to overwhelm his self-control. *If I really let go,* he thought, *I could kill someone without meaning to.* Was it just the 'adolescent emotions' they talked about in Family Living? *I hope so. That doesn't excuse it, but it won't last, it'll go away in a few years.* He resolved to apologize as soon as he got back home.

He looked at his Timex under a street light. Six-thirty, and it should take only twenty minutes to walk to Aspen. *Well, if I'm ten minutes early she shouldn't mind.*

He wondered what Cheshire wanted to see him about. "Something's come up." Something good or something bad? Did she mean Joe's accident?

He crossed the railroad tracks and walked beside them, head down, hands in hispockets, analyzing her tone and her words for subtle shades of meaning. His mind was far away but his feet carried him on steadily toward the newer section of town.

Maybe, just maybe, she felt the same way he did about her. After all, she'd committed a crime to save him from being hurt. He was grateful for that, even if he felt bad for Joe. *But look at it realistically, buds,* he told himself. *He was planning to knife you. If that had been you in that hospital bed, he'd give a rat's ass? I think not.*

His mind drifted back to their one wonderful night. What was it she'd said, standing there so beautiful as he left; that she wasn't really sure yet if she was sorry, or something like that. What a funny thing to say. What did she mean?

He kicked angrily at the gravel on the railbed. *Yeah, she's deep,* he thought. Different from the stupid, mean girls in school. Different from that bitch Alex.

* * *

Cheshire was brushing her hair in the bedroom when she heard a knock on her front door. She put the brush away and went out to the living room. *If that's him, he's certainly punctual,* she thought. "Who is it?" she called, checking herself in the full-length mirror.

124

"Phil. Phil Pirella."

She patted her hair one last time and let him in.

"Wow. You really look nice," he said, awed. She was in a long dress, and had done something different to her hair. At school she always wore a severely cut jacket and a pleated skirt.

"Thanks," she said, surprised at how pleased she felt at his unfeigned admiration. "Have a seat. Want some tea?"

He collapsed onto her sofa, and a moment later she called, from the kitchen, "Or would you rather have something stronger?"

"Whatever you're having's fine with me."

Something shattered in the kitchen. He started to his feet. "Are you okay? Do you need help?" he called.

"No, I'm just cracking the ice. Be right out."

A moment later he had a shallow, frosty glass in his hand, and his fingertips were getting cold. He tasted it tentatively. "Woof. Boy, this is strong."

She seated herself across the room and sipped. "Do you like it? It's a martini."

"Um, it's great," he lied. It was so strong his eyes were watering. "Um, do you have any tissues?"

"On the table. To your left," she said. Then, after a moment, not looking at him, "There are some things I'd better tell you before you hear them from someone else. If, that is, you haven't already."

"What things?"

"First of all, I'm afraid I . . . lost the note you gave me. It was a nice note, by the way. But I lost it, and someone found it."

Oh, Jesus, he thought. "Who by?" he said, then corrected himself. "By whom?"

She laughed, and it sounded very nice. Then she was serious again. "I don't know. But Mr. Ashberne has it now. He confronted me with it this morning."

"Oh, no. Then you're in trouble. Oh, I'm sorry, Cheshire."

"It was my fault for misplacing it. Don't feel badly about writing it. I know it came from your heart. And at first, Phil, at first I didn't like it."

"You didn't like it when I said I loved you?"

"No, I didn't. I guess that's because . . . no one ever told me that before, except one man . . . and he just wanted to go to bed with me that night."

"Oh," he said, and wondered if this unnamed man actually had. "That's not why I said it."

"I know that," she said, and they were both silent for a moment. Then she added, "You weren't at school today."

"I went to the hospital to see Joe. He's not doing so well."

"I know. He's paralyzed. I called the ER as soon as the police let me go last night."

Silence fell again between them. Until she said, "Have you ever been in love before? With a girl your own age?"

He considered. "I guess not," he said slowly. "I thought I was once, but I didn't feel the way I feel now about you."

"How do you feel about me?"

"I think you're wonderful. You're clever and beautiful and good. I always want to be with you, close to you. I wish we could be together forever."

She smiled sadly. "Phil, I'm older than you. Not a great deal, not enough to matter, really, but old enough to be able to see where we're going. That's why I didn't like the idea of your falling in love with me. And why I don't want to fall in love with you."

"I don't blame you," he said humbly. "I'm not much, really, not for you."

"Oh, horseshit," she said indignantly. "Don't ever crawl to a woman like that."

"Oh. All right," he said, confused.

126

"Unfortunately," she said, watching him, "I guess I do, whether I want to or not."

She watched the joy flood his face as he understood. How little it took at his age to make one totally happy! She wished she were seventeen again. Had found someone like him years ago.

She sighed. Got up, and crossed to him, her bony frame graceful for once in the whispering gown. She took the glass from his hand. "Kiss me," she said.

She was patient with his clumsy fingers; laughed at his awe at her nakedness; waited for him, helped him, and when he finally understood, surrendered to her own desire. When they were both done she held him so tightly he cried out. "Stay there," she whispered into his ear, blinking back the hot moisture of tears. "Just stay. Don't leave me yet. I love you; Phil, I love you."

* * *

At precisely eight that same evening Marguerita Schmidt gaveled the assemblage into something approaching order, though a beelike hum of conversation continued. She was nervous about this group. It was so much larger than most of the meetings. Almost all the teachers were here, and three hundred others, an enormous crowd for any public business in town. There was even a reporter taking notes in the front row. She gaveled again and the hum subsided, leaving a breathless, expectant hush.

"Tonight's meeting of the Raymondsville Parent-Teacher Association is declared open. Before we proceed to new business, the minutes of last month's meeting will be read. Reba, will you read the minutes?"

The school secretary stood and read the minutes in a loud, clear voice that carried to all corners of the crowded hall. They were brief, concerned with revision of the student dress code, a request for increased appropriations to enlarge the girls' athletic program, and a few other, more minor matters. She finished and sat down. The minutes were moved, seconded and accepted by voice vote.

"Are there any additions or comments on the issues discussed at last month's meeting?" asked Marguerita.

There were none. The whole auditorium was silent. "Very well. Any new business to discuss?"

Several persons raised their hands, some jumped to their feet, and a hubbub rose. She gaveled it firmly down. "You there, in front, Madam. I'm sorry, I don't recall seeing you here before. Please introduce yourself before you speak."

"I'm Mrs. Gorton, my boy is Dennis, he's a sophomore," she yelled shrilly. "What I want to know is, what are you going to do about this teacher who's giving the boys personal sex education after school hours." The audience laughed but quieted as they saw the chairwoman reach for her gavel. *They're under control, she thought. For now. God, what a mob.* "Mr. Ashberne?" she said, turning to him. "Would you care to respond?"

The principal rose and faced the audience. "Thank you, Madame Chairman. I will be happy to answer to the best of my ability." He cleared his throat solemnly. "The facts in this regrettable matter were brought to my attention only this Wednesday, that is to say, yesterday. I of course immediately took steps to investigate so serious a charge. Such activities cannot for a moment be countenanced in an institution which has as its primary concern, as does Raymondsville High, the molding of young men and women of unimpeachable rectitude and firmness of spirit."

"Damn right, Charlie," someone yelled the rear. The audience tittered. Marguerita glared at the back rows, then back at the principal. "Go on, Mr. Ashberne. Please disregard these bad-mannered interruptions."

"Of course," said Ashberne, "It would not be in the interest of justice or fair play to proceed too hastily. In fact, our contracts specify any question of reprimand or dismissal be thoroughly investigated and then voted on by the School Board. My own part is limited to that of an impartial investigator, then to the execution of the Board's decision. Until this takes place, the progress of the investigation has to be kept confidential, in the interest of the woman involved."

He paused for breath and a dozen voices took advantage. "We want her fired," cried one. "Get her out of our school." Several people at once called, almost together, "Fire her!" "Throw her out!" "Get rid of her! She belongs in jail."

"Nevertheless," Ashberne's unctuous tones rose above the noise, "Nevertheless, I may say that the evidence so far appears incontrovertible. The teacher in question has been suspended from teaching, on my own authority, and her case will go before the Board tomorrow, unless she should resign in the meanwhile."

"Thank you, Mr. Ashberne," said Marguerita loudly. She dared not use her gavel again for fear it would be disregarded. "Quiet, please. Quiet, there in back!"

A large man with bushy gray hair shot to his feet and waved. "Madam Chairman. Mrs. Schmidt!"

"Chief Bradner. You have the floor. But please be brief."

"Thank you. Fellow citizens. As many of you know, I have the honor to serve on your school board. I too heard about the kind of hanky-panky this teacher has been running in your school, with your kids. I promise you two things: first, I will be at the meeting to hear this case tomorrow afternoon; second, that if these rumors are even half true, acting on your behalf, I will make certain this immoral predator will never speak another word in one of our classrooms."

Cries of approval echoed from all quarters of the auditorium.

Marguerita rapped again, hard and long. When the din quieted enough for her to be heard, she said, "I think that for the time being we know all that can be said yet on this subject. The Board, as Chief Bradner has assured us, can be depended on to make the appropriate decision and advise us of the results. The subject is closed. Now, is there any other new business?"

One man held up his hand. "The chair recognizes Mr. Langtree."

"Thank you, Madame Chair. I would like to reopen a subject think received all-too-short consideration last month; *id est*, the unilateral decision by the Curriculum Committee, acting *in camera*, to drop the teaching of Latin."

The *Herald* reporter put away his notepad and left, mingling with a departing crowd no longer interested in the meeting once the 'sex scandal' discussion was over. He'd have just enough time to get it written up for the morning edition.

Another person also rose and slipped out, making herself as inconspicuous as possible. Mary had heard far too much, not from the speakers, but from the chatter of those sitting around her. *Not Phil,* she kept thinking numbly, *not my Philip.*

But she knew it was.

FOURTEEN

Phil read the story the next morning. Since he was getting so far behind in his homework he'd decided to take Friday off too, resolving to reattack his studies viciously over the weekend.

He'd gotten up late, dawdled over breakfast, and finally went out to buy the paper to see if anything of importance was going on in the world.

There was. Cheshire's photograph, *from her college yearbook*, he thought numbly, showing her with longer hair, shared the front page with a dramatic shot of the previous night's PTA meeting, showing dozens of hands raised and Chief Bradner standing with his finger pointed threateningly. This red-hot story ran for two full columns under the headline LOCAL TEACHER ACCUSED IN MISCONDUCT CASE.

He read it rapidly, standing alone in the middle of the living room; Mike was eating lunch at the Grill and Mary had gone shopping. The article nauseated him. The person, male or female, who'd written it made it sound as if Cheshire had seduced every male at the school. Though it never directly said anything against her — everything was 'alleged', 'charged' or even just 'rumored' — it struck him as a thorough and vicious smear. As far as the victim was concerned, since the reporter seemed unsure as to his legal age, he was mentioned only as 'son of a well-known town employee and apparently a chronic troublemaker in and out of class.'

He threw the dirty thing on the floor in disgust, then thought better of it and took it into the back yard, pausing for matches. He burned it in the rusty 55-gallon oil drum Jake used as an incinerator.

His mother usually didn't read the paper, and if it wasn't on CBS at seven o'clock, it wasn't news as far as she knew. *Maybe I can spare her this for a few more days at least,* he thought, watching the flames devour Cheshire's face. *The way she is, she'll blame herself for everything.*

When the last scraps of newsprint were crisping and writhing, the telephone rang. He poked the ashes to powder with a stick and went inside. "Pirella residence," he said.

"Phil?" A woman's voice, but not Mary's or Alex's or Cheshire's. In fact, he didn't recognize it at all. "Who is this?" he asked suspiciously.

"Reba, Mr. Ashberne's secretary. Is this Phil?"

Uh oh, he thought. "Yeah, it's me. I'm not feeling good today. I'm sorry, I forgot to call in."

"I don't blame you. I read today's paper too. It's a real hatchet job. Miss M. doesn't deserve that. But that isn't why I called. The School Board's meeting at two. They want to hear from you. Can you come?"

"I guess. Sure. Where do they meet?"

"The conference room. Check in with me. Okay?"

"Okay. Thanks." He hung up. He looked at his watch; high noon. He decided to have something to eat before he got dressed for the meeting. A toasted cheese or two would go down well. But when he'd made and eaten them they formed an indigestible lump.

He dressed neatly in his brown slacks, a white long-sleeved

shirt, and a blue blazer, the only dress coat he owned. *Should I wear at tie? Or would that look as if I'm trying to ingratiate myself?* On the other hand, most of the male members were local businessmen; they'd be in coat and tie. They're expecting a real JD in denim and black leather, if they believe what they read in the paper. Well, I'll play the game their way.

As he went through the unfamiliar motions of tying the tie he remembered the last time he'd dressed up, tried to make a good impression. With Alex. *Well, I'll try not to slap any of them,* he thought, jerking viciously at the knot with one hand, *No matter what they call me. But I won't take any crap about Cheshire, or say anything bad about her.* He imagined himself defending her with golden phrases, reducing the Board to shame.

No, they could do what they wanted with him; they hadn't done anything to be ashamed of. In fact, if it wasn't required for med school, they could cram their precious school. Why should he value a secondary diploma from a town so full of vengeful, petty people? Oh, to hell with this tie. He couldn't do it alone, not with one hand. He jerked the abortive knot apart and threw the thing back in his drawer.

He got there on time and checked in at Reba's cubicle. She wasn't there, but another woman was. "Where's Reba?" he asked.

"She's steno-ing the Board meeting," said the girl. "She said that when – you're Pirella, right?"

"Right."

"Good, you're to wait outside the conference room until she comes out for you. There's someone else in there now."

"Thanks." He followed her and took a seat. He picked up the August copy of *Reader's Digest* but couldn't follow any of the articles.

Reba called him in at two-thirty. "Philip Pirella," she said to the people in the conference room, sitting down again at her own little table. Phil stood, facing eight older men – no, two middle-aged women as well – seated around a long table. The only one he recognized was Chief Bradner, but he made no sign of recognition, although he'd often seen Phil at the station with Jake.

The oldest-looking member, a wizened guy with scanty white hair carefully combed back over his scalp, leaned back in his chair and studied Phil. "Pirella," he said. "I've heard your name before, and in none to savory a context. And now this mess."

Phil noted that this man, who seemed by his bearing to be the leader, wore a dark-blue tie with a silver monogrammed H. He said, "If you're Mr. Heckathorn, sir, you probably heard my name from Alicia Ryan or her dad. The story she was telling, though, isn't entirely true."

Heckathorn's small gray eyes grew even colder. "We're not discussing that case just now. But yes, Alex told me, privately, what you did to her, or tried to. I know her well. She tells the truth, no matter what the cost to herself. That's what I need from you, young man, even if it's only once in your life, about this thing with the Marzeau woman."

"Yes, sir," said Phil weakly. Heckathorn's icy gaze seemed to drain his confidence. He had the feeling this old man could see through him, and wasn't impressed with what he saw.

"Now," said Heckathorn, flicking at a piece of paper on the table, "This note. You wrote it to Miss Marzeau, your AP teacher. Correct?"

"Yes, sir."

"Mrs. Schmidt, Mrs. Sankner, forgive me if I speak bluntly and to the point, but I want to save us all time and make the facts clear. How many times have you and Miss Marzeau had sexual relations?"

Phil flushed but kept control of his tongue. It sounded so dirty the way the old man mouthed the words. "Twice."

"Only twice? Since when?"

"The first time was Tuesday. The second was yesterday."

A few of the other members made notes on the pads in front of them. Heckathorn did not. He held Phil's eyes with a hard, level, evaluating gaze. "Thank you for being forthright. You understand, Phil, this is not a crime Cheshire Marzeau is being accused of. You are of age. In this state, at least. At most, she'll be dismissed and given an unfavorable evaluation. We aren't out to crucify anyone. But we can't allow things like this to happen in our schools. Relationships of this kind can be very dangerous to adolescents, emotionally and in other ways. Can you understand our position?"

"I guess," he mumbled.

"Knowing this, then, have you anything to add to your previous remarks?"

"No, sir."

"Anything you yourself would like to say to us?"

"No, sir," he muttered, wanting nothing so much as to be out of there.

"All right. Only two more questions and we'll be done. First, was there any element of coercion in Marzeau's approach to you? Did she threaten, say, to give you bad grades if you didn't sleep with her?"

"It wasn't like that at all," he said, shocked from his intimidation by the lowness of the charge. "It just sort of happened one night. It was raining, when I went – "

"Please," said Heckathorn, holding up a hand wearily to stop him. "Spare us the details. I'm sure all our members have lived long enough to know how things like that can happen. But I had to ask. Finally, to the best of your knowledge, have any other students or other teachers been involved in this kind of sexual activity?"

"No."

"I'm glad to hear that, at any rate." He turned to the others.

"Do the other members have any additional questions for this witness?"

They didn't, and he was allowed to leave. He walked out into the main office again and headed for the door. But the woman at Reba's desk called him back. "I have a letter here from Mr. Ashberne for you. I was to give it to you after you saw the Board."

"Thanks." He tore open the long white official-looking envelope. It was a notice of suspension. It didn't say for how long. The principal had signed it with a flourish at the bottom. *Gee*, he thought, *I can take this home and frame it instead of a diploma.*

He went to his locker and took out all his books and notebooks, leaving the door open. He lugged the pile down to the track room and threw it in the bottom of his cross-country locker. He wasn't clear whether suspension from classes meant he couldn't use the gym. He probably wouldn't be allowed to represent the school at meets. But since he never got to run at meets anyway, that wasn't much of a cross to bear.

Maybe a run will take things off my mind, he thought.

* * *

The church was empty except for Mary. She'd been kneeling at the statue of the Virgin, a votive candle burning before her in the still air, for ever so long; her knees were going numb, but still she prayed on, her lips moving automatically in the comforting words as her heart struggled with anguish. *Therefore I beseech blessed Mary, ever virgin, holy Michael the archangel, Peter and Paul and all the saints. . . .*

Oh God, she thought, mingled with the rushing of the worn prayers through her mind, *please save my son, as dear to me as Yours was to You. Forgive me, forgive me for my sin . . . through my fault, through my fault . . .* and her mind slipped back through the years, *mea culpa, mea culpa, mea maxima culpa.*

What can I do? she implored Mother Mary silently, wringing her hands.

The statue smiled down at the kneeling woman, both figures dim in the flickering candlelight. *Mary, so often I have prayed you to intercede for me, thy namesake, oh Mother of God, and you have brought ne comfort and relief in my sorrow at the greatness of my sin. Now I ask your intercession not for myself but for my son, tempted to mortal sin by an evil woman. How can I help him?*

Presently, a long time later, the prayers died from her lips as she finally understood what she had to do.

* * *

Phil dressed out alone in the locker room. He jogged out into the sunlight and did a short, half-hearted warmup in the middle of the empty field. It was unseasonably warm and he broke a sweat easily. Hearing the final bell inside, he lurched into motion, leaving the track behind as he headed out Maple.

The day was almost perfectly calm; only the faintest breath of breeze moved, from behind him, so he ran in the same pocket of air, as if on a treadmill. The unyielding pavement reawakened the pain in his lower legs that had bothered him since he started road workouts. *Not again*, he thought wearily.

Well, it would pass. Or, more accurately, the pain in lungs and thighs would blot out the lesser stabs of discomfort from the shin splints. Crap; in his haste he'd forgotten a dose of talcum powder in his supporter. His thighs would be rubbed raw on a day like today. But he kept on out of town, sweat running down his forehead and dripping into his eyes. He'd left his pants in his locker, but the sweatshirt was roasting him.

So now I'm suspended, indefinitely, he thought. For bad conduct, presumably, or some even more damning phrase like 'moral turpitude'. And it'd go as part of his transcript to whatever college he tried to get into, ever. *Most guys in my situation*, he thought, *could enlist. Serve as a corpsman or medic, maybe eventually get into a service-funded med school.* Not him. Not with the useless arm curled against his chest. His dreams of being a doctor looked farther away ever.

Except for Jake and Mary, there's really nothing tying me to this shitty town. No warm childhood memories. No hope of a brighter future. No real friends. Except for Carl, yeah, and maybe Myrna.

And Cheshire, above all, Cheshire. *For her*, he thought, *I could stay here and take everything they'd pile on me.* But they'd never let her stay. In a town this small, no one would dare hire her.

Right turn, uphill. The heat seemed to focus on him as he left the grass-lined sidewalks behind for the open road.

No question, he'd have to decide soon. He couldn't stay in limbo, studying at home, missing tests, struggling not to fall too far behind. And they could make it permanent anytime they wanted, just dismiss him.

Maybe he should just bite the bullet. Blow town and trust to luck. Get a job somewhere else and finish his education where he'd be anonymous and unknown. It would be hard, but at least everyone wouldn't hate him, wouldn't be against him, as they always would be here.

And Cheshire? He honestly couldn't see them letting her stay on. But surely a quiet resignation could have been arranged. The way they were treating her was more like a witch hunt.

Reaching the top of the rise outside town, he started down the bare, hot asphalt. Pools of illusory water shimmered on the pavement ahead, winking out as he neared.

Yeah, he thought. *I have some left in the bank from birthday presents and last summer's work at the doughnut shop.* He'd draw it tomorrow and leave.

And where, with a few hundred bucks, an unfinished high-school education, and a withered arm, where could he go? He pondered that as he let the grade carry him downward toward the logging road turnoff, though he suspected there was only one answer.

He needed someplace with both anonymity and opportunity. The former, so their relationship wouldn't be questioned; the latter, because he'd need to eat. That meant there was only one place to go. There'd be something for him, no matter how obscure and menial at first, in New York City. *I'll try for something like a hospital orderly first*, he thought, warming to the idea of making his own way in the city small-towners envied and hated. *But if that's not open, anything else. I can finish school by mail order, or night classes.* And after that, wasn't there a free college in New York City? Any job would do, he'd make it do, as long as he could leave Raymondsville far behind, never to be thought of again until the years and his successes sweetened the bitter memories.

And Cheshire will go with me!

With this last thought he stopped running. Why go on? It was futile. He wasn't on the team anymore. He had no right to be wearing this sweatshirt, these red-and-gold shorts.

He turned round and began to walk back along the road, then angled off into a field and took a shortcut through a scrubby patch of second-growth woods. Here, at least, it was cool, and now he was walking into the light breeze. It dried his sweaty face and he relished the slight chill on his bare legs.

When he got back to the gym most of the other guys had arrived, changed, and gone out on their workouts. Saarlo came over as he began to strip off, throwing his sweats in the laundry bin for the last time. "Need a hand, Phil?" Carl asked.

He looked up, surprised. The first time another student had spoken to him in a week. *Good old Carl*, he thought. *He was the first to warn me about Alex, and try to give me advice; and now here he was again, talking to me like a pal.* He'd remember Carl long after he forgot Raymondsville existed."Yeah, thanks," he said with a quiet smile.

"I heard about the suspension," his friend said as he pulled the sopping sweatshirt off. "A lot of the guys think you got shafted. Some of em're starting to feel sorry they were so hard on you before."

"I didn't care," Phil said. "I guess I won't be running with them anymore, though."

"Sure you will. How long's your suspension?"

"Indefinite. But the way Heckathorn, he's the big cheese, talked, I think indefinite's gonna mean forever."

"B.S. They can't. It's all Marzeau's fault. Sorry, Phil, I know you like her, but it's the teacher's bad when anything like this happens. They're only trying to throw a scare into you with this suspension so you'll be a good little boy when you come back. It won't last a week."

"Maybe," said Phil. "And maybe they'll ask me back and I won't be here."

Carl laughed at that. "Yeah, that'd serve 'em right, Doc."

Apparently he had a new nickname. He liked it better than 'crip.' "Anyway, I'm glad you decided to talk to me again. And I appreciate the way you tried to get people to see my side. You're a real friend, Carl."

"Hell. I was wrong to stop talking to you in the first place; I'm ashamed I did. If Ryan'd ever go out with me she'd have to fight me off. They shouldn't blame a guy for trying . . . Look, I only had a sprint workout. Why don't we grab a beer at Willy's tonight? Or the Hive?"

"I don't see why not," Phil said. "Just let me call home and let them know where I am. Got wheels?"

"My 125 and a spare helmet," Saarlo said. "To the showers. Thank God, it's Friday.'"

The Hill

* * *

Willy's was crowded. Scores of kids from all over Hemlock County jammed the low wooden building, perched on the hoods of cars, drank, laughed, talked. Loud music, spilling into the road from the open door, relieved those inside from the need to talk. But for most purposes a raised, empty glass, a smile, a kiss or a feel sufficed. The evening was young and more people arrived every hour.

Ray Corrigan, the self-appointed life of every party, was regaling the cross-country contingent, sitting under the stars at the outdoor bar in back, with old drinking songs, of which he knew dozens. Most of the team members had drifted in during the course of the evening and had, after a few beers, been corraled by Saarlo and led to the back.

By midnight everyone was thoroughly snockered, especially Phil, and the stage of good fellowship with all the world had been reached. As Carl had probably intended. At first Phil had hung back, saying little but covering it by drinking steadily. He felt sad. *This'll be the last time*, he thought, *I'll be at Willy's Friday night with the guys.* The loud good-fellowship, the joking and horseplay, the heavy bass beat of the live rock, the well-known voices in the dim light from the windows, all made him conscious he'd miss it. It was a bittersweet feeling, but it didn't shake his resolve. He was leaving, and good riddance.

As time passed., the party developed into an impromptu salute to Joe, who'd been a fixture here on Fridays. Little by little, without a clear-cut time when he could say it happened, Phil was reaccepted. He wasn't forgiven, or even asked about things. It wasn't mentioned. He was, very simply, asked to pass the chips.

Well past midnight, Steve Rapisjek had been out in the

141

darkness, unwilling for some reason to use the Willy's can, and when he came back his big hand almost pitched Phil out of his chair as it came down on his shoulder. Phil, who could barely sit up, turned drunkenly. "Phil," he said, "Sorry I din't talk to you. We're buddies, right?" It was the longest speech anyone had ever heard him make and they all laughed as Phil and Steve shook hands in drunken solemnity. Phil started to topple and Carl propped him up.

But it was getting late, and Willy was turning the lights out inside. "Phil?" said Carl. "Ready to make tracks, man?"

No answer. Corrigan bent to peer under the table. "He's out cold under there. He's been partying hearty all night."

"Christ," said Saarlo. He stood up, weaving. "I can't take him home on a Honda if the sonofabitch can't hold on."

"Anyone riding with you," said Corrigan, "should be dead drunk, or else crazy."

They allguffawed, but laughed even louder when Carl, watching for his chance, tipped Ray's chair with his foot and he crashed backward, screaming.

"I'll take him," Rapisjek said. "My truck."

Willy came out back and yelled that he was calling the cops. They called him a spoilsport and a chocolate-coated bastard but left grudgingly, forgetting Phil.

Belatedly, after he started his truck, Rapisjek remembered and left it running and went back to get him. He pulled Phil out from under the table and onto his feet, and piloted him out. "In the bed," he grunted, and helped Phil over the gate.

At Phil's house he parked, let down the gate, swearing under his breath, and tried to wake Phil up. *Christ, the kid don't hold his beer too good,* he thought fuzzily. He'd have to hose the bed out in the morning. Good thing he hadn't put him in the cab. Unable to rouse him, at last he picked him up bodily and carried him up the walk. The porch light was on and the door unlocked. He stumbled in as quietly as he could, dumped his burden on the floor, and weaved out.

Not such a loser after all, he thought. *Christ, imagine banging an English teacher.*

That took guts.

FIFTEEN

O h, Jeez," he groaned aloud when at last he awoke. He wanted to stay in bed but his bladder was about to burst. Throwing back the covers, he tried to sit up. The throbbing in his head became a repetitive agony. His mouth was dry. His eyes were gummed blind. He felt sick to his stomach. "Jesus," he whispered, and put his head between his knees. It helped, but not much.

Finally he staggered up, reeling, and padded into the bathroom, catching a glimpse of his clock in passing. One in the afternoon. The house was quiet.

Bladder relieved, he drank deeply from the faucet, cupping his good hand to form a little pool. The cold water made him feel sick again, but it stayed down, as did the two aspirin.

That should help, he thought. He went back to bed and lay down again very carefully, sighing as his head settled into the pillow. He was no longer sleepy, but it hurt less lying down.

He flinched, suddenly wondering, *How did I get back here last night? How did I get upstairs?* He puzzled this over for some minutes. There was a vague memory of being jolted around in the bed of a truck. Whose truck? He couldn't remember. The last thing he could recover with any clarity was singing some drinking song with the rest of the guys at Willy's.

He gave up on it for the time being, but stayed in bed, drifting in and out of a doze until three, when his mother came home from shopping. She opened his door a crack and looked in."Phil?" she whispered."Are you up?"

"Hi, Mom."

She came in and closed the door and sat on the edge of his bed."Are you feeling all right now?" she asked in a worried voice. "We found you asleep on the living room floor. Where were you last night?"

"Some of the guys on the team were down at Willy's. We had a great time. I'll be all right in a little while."

She shook her head. "Well, you never drank this much before, so I guess you had to find out what it's like. Just so you don't make a habit of it. Doesn't feel very good right now, does it?"

"Nope. I don't think I'll do that again."

"That's a good resolution," said Mary approvingly. But she couldn't help remembering the many times she'd said that herself. She remembered the terrible drunken lonely days, and shuddered inwardly. *Dear God*, she thought, *forgive me and guard my boy.*

"You have to be careful the way you live, and the things you do, Philly. Too many kids your age think living's only for thrills, and they try to find them in drugs, and sex, and liquor. There's more to life, no matter what the TV and the books at school and the other boys say. The only things that really matter are your good health, your soul, and the people who love you." She patted him on the good arm. "I want you to have a good life, son. You've always been a good boy, Philly. It hurts me to see you doing something you'll be ashamed of later."

I'm not ashamed of it, he thought, but he couldn't say that to his mother, his doggedly religious mother who saw everything as right or wrong, good or bad, grace or sin. She'd never understand how he felt about Cheshire. But aloud he said nothing, just closed his eyes.

He's not listening, she thought sadly. *He'll learn. But only in his own time. And someday he'll try to tell someone something and they won't listen either.*

But this was scant comfort and she finally rose and started to leave, then turned back quickly. "Do you feel like eating anything? I'll bring it up if you want. Some creamed chipped beef, on toast?"

"That sounds good, Mom," he said. "Thanks."

She left. He sat up again, experimentally. His head felt a little better, probably from the aspirin. His stomach growled, and he was suddenly ravenous. He threw on a bathrobe and had another long drink of water, then went downstairs to spare his mother the trouble of carrying it up.

The chipped beef and toast were delicious. He had six pieces of toast, grape juice, and Mary made him drink some black coffee, though he'd never liked its bitter, thick taste. After his meal he went into the living room and turned the television on. He sat down in Jake's recliner and stretched. "Say, Mom, where's Jake?" he called.

"He went in today," she said from the kitchen. "Bill Oliver was out sick and Chief told the sergeant to call Jake."

"That's good," he said, getting up to change the channels. Television bored him. Sports, nothing but sports. *I like to run,* he thought, *but watching other people play golf doesn't turn me on.* That was all that was on Saturday afternoon, though. And in the evening nothing but crime shows. Last year nothing but doctors. When he was little, westerns. *Why not a little variety,* he thought. Finally he turned it off and reached for a magazine.

That too failed to interest and he sat dithering dejectedly. Then got up, went to the telephone, and dialed Cheshire's number. It rang but no one answered.

Well, it was getting late. He might as well go to the bank before it closed.

Jake let himself in. He was in uniform. "Is that him?" Mary called.

"I'm home, hon," Jake called. He unbuckled his belt and took out his worn Model 10 and unloaded it, putting the nickeled cartridges back in the belt loops one by one.

"I see they gave you back the badge, Dad," Phil said.

"Not really."

"You're not back on the force?"

"Sort of." His stepdad sounded tired. "Bradner says officially I'm still suspended.But they're shorthanded because of the flu, so they're sort of using me part-time."

"That's too bad," Phil said. Thinking, *But once I'm gone they'll take him back. He won't suffer from my mistakes anymore.* "Say, how late's the drive-through open at the bank? It stays open late, doesn't it?"

"On Saturday? 'Til five, I think . . . what's the idea getting so drunk? I had to carry you up and put you to bed. And your clothes were filthy."

"I know," he said humbly. "I was out with the guys. I guess I just didn't know when to stop."

"Well, now you do," grumbled Jake, but let it drop. He turned on the TV and was instantly absorbed. "Jeez, didja see that pass!"

"That's really something," said Phil, and went upstairs to change.

Dressed, he got the little green bank book out of his metal box. He tucked it in his pocket and began to pull on his track jacket, but changed his mind and discarded it for a pullover. After another long pull of cold water he went back downstairs and started out the front door.

"Phil?" His mother, who'd come in. "Where are you going?"

"Just downtown."

She must have caught the evasion in his tone. "You're not going to see that woman again, are you?"

That woman. "No, Mom."

"Are you sure?"

"Yeah, I'm sure. I probably won't see her again for, um, some time. If ever."

"That's good," she said, still sounding unconvinced. "You go on, but don't stay out too late. I guess you had your supper already. And Phil, please . . . don't see her again."

He bared his teeth. "Did you hear me say I wasn't?"

"All right, Phil, all right," she said hastily.

* * *

"Hullo, Phil," said the teller, a small, fussy fellow who knew him through his stepdad; Jake often escorted him to the plywood plant on paydays, and once or twice Phil had tagged along. "What can I do for ya today?"

"Closing my account, Mr. Petersen. Need the cash."

"Sure. I'll keep the account open for you, though, so you won't have to open a new one next time you come back."

"Don't bother," Phil said.

"What? You leaving town or something?" Petersen said, sounding surprised.

It would be nasty if the teller got the idea he was running away. He could call Jake and that'd be a nasty scene, especially if his mom got involved. *I want to leave quietly,* he thought. *It'll be easier for everybody that way.* "I guess you're right, Mr. Petersen. Leave it open. I'll keep my bankbook."

When he had the cash in a tight roll in his pocket he crossed the street to the Greyhound terminal, which shared a room with a small travel agency, and bought a one-way ticket to New York

City. "How much luggage can I take?" he asked the clerk, a guy he didn't know, thank God.

"Sixty pounds in the luggage compartment and two pieces of hand luggage. Whatever's in the luggage compartment'll be checked through to Penn Station. You won't have to worry about it when you transfer."

"Okay. When's the next bus?"

"Evening bus, nine-fifteen PM tomorrow. You'll get there a little after seven A.M. Changes at Hammondsport and Binghamton. Here's a schedule."

"Thanks." He pocketed the ticket and schedule. "See ya tomorrow."

He spent his last evening in Raymondsville walking around the streets as dark fell, remembering.

* * *

Cheshire was spending Saturday at home. The phone had rung several times, but after listening to too many abusive and threatening callers, she didn't answer it anymore. So she let it ring and sat alone in her bare apartment with Wolfe curled beside her and tried to read. Though it wasn't going very well. *It can't be the book*, she thought. It was a new novel by one of her favorites, just discovered and published posthumously, and she knew like all his books it was tremendously exciting and wonderfully well written. So it must be her. She laid it aside and played with Wolfe, scratching his head while the white cat closed its eyes in pleasure.

Presently she shooed him out of her lap and tried to interest herself in a soap opera. But the characters' problems seemed trivial and contrived. *Maybe because my own seem so much more important,* she thought. A soap could only interest someone with a settled, unexciting life. *And my life – since I met Phil, at any rate --*

is anything but.

She'd decided to get drunk, and was in fact pouring herself the first glass of wine, when a knock at her door made her start, spilling a few drops on the sideboard. "Just a moment," she called, mopping the spill up hurriedly. "Who is it?"

"Mrs. Pirella. Philip's mother."

Oh, God, she thought, closing her eyes in agony. *Not now. I can't take a fight with his mother now on top of everything else. I can't, my nerves won't take it.* She yelled, "What do you want?"

"To talk," came through the heavy door. "I'm alone."

Cheshire went to her door and opened it a bit, leaving the chain fastened, and looked out at the woman. She didn't look too threatening. "I don't think we have much to say to each other, Mrs. Pirella," she said through the crack.

"Maybe you don't. But I think I have a right to see what kind of a woman my son is mixed up with."

"Well, you've seen me," said Cheshire, not without hostility. "Now go away."

"No. Let me in. I only want to talk."

"I'm not in the mood, Mrs. Pirella. I'm really very upset."

"How do you think I feel? Now let me in. We need to settle some things."

She saw at last that the woman was determined to get in, she wasn't going to leave until she did, and after a moment more she closed the door and unrattled the chain. "Come in," she said grudgingly. "Go ahead. Sit down."

Mary sat without speaking and silently they took each other's measure.

Cheshire spoke first, eager to terminate the interview as quickly as she could. "Now, just what was it you wanted to say to me, Mrs. Pirella?"

Now she was inside the apartment Phil's mother seemed less inclined to come to the point. Her curious glance examined each part of the room in turn, then focused on her with the same intense interest. At last she said, "You don't look like what I expected."

Cheshire laughed shortly. "You expected some cheap, sexy little thing, I imagine. Sorry to disappoint. Well, you came here to call me a whore. Go ahead, I'm ready."

Mary was puzzled. This woman neither looked nor acted like the tramp she'd expected, the kind who used their bodies to get what they wanted. She was young, but not pretty. *In fact,* she thought, *When I was her age I was much better looking.*

"Why?" she said. "Why did you do it? What did my boy have for you?"

Cheshire was taken aback. This woman didn't scream or make threats. She'd only asked an anguished question in a normal, human tone. She relaxed her guard, but stayed wary. "Have for me? What do you mean?"

"What did you get out of it? What's he ever done to you?" Then, remembering how this woman had hurt him, she cried, "Why did you do it? Answer me!"

"I don't know," said Cheshire weakly. "I didn't mean to. I was lonely, I needed someone. Haven't you ever done anything you knew was wrong, but you had to, just because?"

"But if you knew it was wrong," Mary started, then the last sentence the other had spoken hit her and she stopped, shaken. She turned white and bit at her lip.

"Are you all right?" asked Cheshire, her hostility forgotten. The older woman looked very unwell indeed.

Mary buried her face in her hands and began to sob.

She's not well, Cheshire thought. And sat still until the other woman should stop crying.

At last Mary caught her breath. She opened her purse and dabbed at her nose and eyes with a Kleenex. "I guess I get it," she said. "Once, I was lonely and needed someone too. I found him, but too late to stop me from doing something terribly wrong to – to another person. That's a story you don't need to hear. But I can understand loneliness. And how it can drive people to do crazy things."

"I see." Cheshire didn't, not really. "Are you sure you're all right, then?"

"Oh, I'll live. But you listen to me now. Between you and Phil. It can't go on. you know that, don't you? You mustn't see him again. Nothing good can come of it. You do see that, don't you?"

"Yes, Mrs. Pirella," said Cheshire Marzeau, sitting very straight and prim and unlovely in her lonely apartment. "I do. I know that."

When she was gone Thomas Wolfe jumped back to his place on his mistress's lap, and the cat's great eyes blinked as her tears soaked into his white fur.

* * *

Sitting at the town bus stop, waiting to go home, Mary was conscious of an overwhelming sadness, but as for a thing long past; and also of feeling purged, relieved. *He's gone now*, she thought. *Philly, my little boy, whom I carried so badly. I hope I've made up for that, raising him.*

Yes, I was lonely too then, she thought, *but my escape was in drink, not running around with men. After Phil's father I never thought I'd want another man in my life. But then I met Jacob. And though I felt guilty every time I looked at Phil, I've never been lonely since.*

"I guess Philly was lonely, too," she whispered to herself. Looking for someone, and couldn't find anyone his own age, because of his arm. *Well, I don't know*, she thought, looking back over her life. *Things happen, because we're weak. We're human. Some drink too much and some steal and some sleep around. And we're all guilty, all of us, full of too much guilt and not enough love.*

Sitting there alone on the hard green-painted bench at the street corner she remembered the sweet, forgiving smile of the Virgin and thought, *Only people need a forgiving God. Only people, because in all the world we're the only creatures who can imagine perfection yet never attain it. And for that we can't forgive ourselves. We needed Your Son.*

And at that she smiled, this aging woman sitting alone on the streetcorner, because she remembered that after all, though in different words, that was exactly what the good nuns had told her so long ago, when she was ten.

SIXTEEN

Five changes of underwear should be adequate. He folded his shorts and t-shirts very small to leave room for the rest of his things. His clothes could all go in the large suitcase, in the Greyhound's luggage compartment. He riffled through the mass of clothing, mostly outgrown or worn-out, that was crammed into his closet, searching for things he could wear in the City.

I hope Mike or Mary doesn't decide to come up here, he thought, and latched his door from the inside to give himself a few seconds to hide everything in case they did. They shouldn't, though; they'd all three returned from twelve o'clock mass a little while before, and his parents seemed to have settled down in the living room to read the Sunday paper and knit while he went upstairs. Now, a capacious, well-used old suitcase gaped on his bed, with a small athletic bag empty beside it.

It's hard to know what to take, he thought. *Though I don't actually have that much.* Maybe three pair of trousers and four or five shirts. His wool pullover, and another one with a V-neck Mary had knitted the year before. His blue blazer, really too small for him now, but he'd need it for job interviews. He'd buy a clip-on tie, so he wouldn't need help. Raincoat and hat.

That filled the suitcase. He closed and locked it, and set it on the floor. It would be unwieldy, but not heavy enough to be unmanageable. The hard part would be getting it down to the station. But how could he carry two pieces of luggage with one arm? Put one on his back?

That triggered an idea, and he searched the recesses of his closet until he found his old Boy Scout pack. It was moth-eaten and faded, but the buckles and straps were still on it. *I guess it'll do. I'll leave the athletic bag and take the pack.*

He loaded it with toothbrush, soap, the razor he'd used once, a few clean handkerchiefs, and a towel and washcloth. From the box under his bed came a few photographs, the condoms, the now-valueless bankbook, and the *U.S. Army Handbook of General Medicine,* which he'd found in a used bookstore and read dozens of times. There were a few other things in the box he didn't intend to take and he picked each up in turn, impressing it on his memory. Then he relocked the box and shoved it back into its dark privacy under his bed.

He went downstairs into the kitchen. His parents were both still in the living room and the dialogue from the TV was broken only occasionally by their low conversation. I twas very quiet in the house, and outside, in the street, few cars passed. It was midafternoon and in Raymondsville most people still passed Sunday quietly.

He rifled the cupboards stealthily, taking things that would keep without refrigeration; a jar of smoked chipped beef, a bag of chocolate chips, an Italian sausage, two cans of tuna, some peanut brittle. *That'll hold me for the trip,* he thought, *maybe even a day or two after I get there. No telling how long before I can find a job.*

Upstairs again with his booty, he spilled everything out of the pack and restowed it, placing *General Medicine* where it would present a flat surface to his back and the tins and other dense objects at the bottom. Can opener? He went back downstairs for one. A jackknife. Matches? No, that was silly, he wouldn't be a tramp in the woods.

But it would be winter soon, and he could expect to do some walking. He got his overcoat out of the closet and shook the mothballs out of the pockets. It was too bulky to pack. It would hot but he'd wear it until he boarded. It was a heavy wool red-and-black-checked hunting coat Mary had found at a church rummage sale. *I'll look like a hick wearing this in the Big Apple*, he thought with disgust. But there was nothing else warm that still fitted him. *So I look like a hick, well, that's what I'll be for a while.* He stuffed gloves into the pockets.

He looked around with surprise. He was packed. How few of the things he owned would accompany him to a new life! All his old clothes, that Mary had bought and kept clean and repaired for him, now worn and outgrown; his books, that he'd scrounged and searched out and bought at yard sales and used bookstores on Cooper Street; the airplane and ship models, with so much care and love invested when he'd been twelve and thirteen, now sitting dusty on a shelf; his smelly old ball glove, bat, football, the .22 rifle Jake had given him. And on the wall rack with it, the relics of his longest battle; the cane, the crutch, the shiny axle of the chair he was to have been always bound to. The toothmarks on the cane brought back memories of Ralph, and of how the poor mutt had died, run over on the street by a car that had never stopped.

So many memories, bound up with these familiar things! Jake had helped him bury the dog's stiff little body on the slope of a hill overlooking the town, in a grove of young pines so in years to come they'd cover the grave with aromatic needles.

At the thought of death he remembered his parents. They too might die while he was gone. Oh, sure, he'd write, maybe even visit after a while; it wasn't that far, three hundred miles or so. But this was the parting, the leaving of the nest. *Wish I could say goodbye,* he thought, eyes stinging a little. *But I'll leave a note. They won't worry so much then, and by the time they read it, it'll be too late to stop me.*

Crouching over his study table, he jotted a short note explaining that he was leaving, why, and that he'd be all right and would write after he was settled in. He didn't say where he was going. He closed with a few words of thanks and love to them both, and sat at the desk for a few moments blinking back new tears. Then stuffed it into an envelope and licked the seal. *I'll leave it in the mailbox,* he thought. *There's no delivery on Sundays so Mom won't check it 'til tomorrow morning. By then I'll be long gone.*

He set the suitcase, pack, and coat aside, then went about the room rearranging it to look normal again. *I'll eat dinner and then leave,* he thought, keeping his mind fixed on the mechanics to prevent his emotions taking over. He felt sad about leaving Jake and Mary, but it was for the best. *Like Lord Jim,* he thought. *To the destructive element commit myself, and by struggle, force it to bear me up. And I will, by God, I'll make it on my own.* Behind his sadness and bitterness, excitement was growing.

"This time tomorrow I'll be there," he whispered, and sitting on his bed thought for a while, anticipating, imagining.

"Dinner," his mother called. He became conscious of a blend of delicious smells rising from below.

"Be right down, Mom," he shouted back, folding the envelope and slipping it into his pocket. With a last glance around he went downstairs.

"There's mashed potatoes," Mary said as she passed bread and Jake carved thin pieces of roast beef. "And horseradish in this little bowl, and mustard too. Phil, we have potato chips in the pantry, I forgot to bring them out."

When he came back with the chips the beef was ready, plenty of it, red and steaming on a heated plate. Mary had made brown gravy from the drippings and it was on the table in a covered

157

bowl. She always set the table with a white linen tablecloth and her best dishes on Sunday. This happened every week, but today he noted every detail, the good smell of the hot food, the ornate silver from their wedding that his mother polished every month, Jake's obvious enjoyment of the plain but substantial food and his glass of cold beer, his mother's frequent glances to see if either of them needed anything. "This is real good, Mom," he said earnestly. He had to take a drink of milk in order to swallow because his throat was a little tight. He took out a handkerchief to blow his nose.

"Go easy on that horseradish, son," said Jake between bites of his second helping.

They had vanilla ice cream with nuts and something different Mary had bought, Nesselrode sauce, after supper. She made coffee, but Phil turned that down. Then, on second thought, accepted. "With sugar and milk, please, Mom. Lots of sugar," he said.

When everything had been eaten and the dishes had been cleared away and he was full, he went up to his room and took the letter out of his pocket and held it in his hand for a few minutes. Then he went downstairs and out to the porch.

When he opened the mailbox to put his note in there were three letters inside. *No one checked the mail last night*, he thought. One was to Mr. Jacob Pirella, from the power company, and the other two were for him.

The long official-looking envelope was from the high school. The other was smaller, squarer, a pink envelope. He recognized Cheshire's handwriting, which he'd seen on the blackboard. It had no stamp. She'd been here, left it in their mailbox herself. That was odd.

He laid the electric bill and his own note aside and, sitting down on the front steps, opened the one from the high school.

It was from Mr. Ashberne. Phil's suspension was terminated.

He was to report to school again as of Monday week. If he desired extra tutoring to make up for the material he'd missed, he was directed to speak to the teacher concerned, or in the case of Senior English, to Mrs. Carzie, who'd be teaching that subject until a qualified replacement could be found.

He laid that aside and tore open the letter from Cheshire. His hands were trembling. It was getting too dark to read on the porch and he walked over to the street light and sat down with his back against the pole, legs folded Indian-fashion. Her note was short. Dear Phil, it started. He read it through twice.

When he had finished it the second time, he folded the note carefully and tucked it back in the envelope. He took the letters back into the house and left the bill and the reinstatement on the kitchen table.

Going up to his room, he pulled on his tennis shoes and left the house again. The note to his parents and her letter were still in his jeans pocket.

It was very dark outside the circles of light from the streetlamps. The moon would be up later, but right now it was very dark. He started to jog down Redwood, heading west. A cool breeze was blowing from behind him, toward the darkness ahead. The streets were quiet, the soles of his shoes making a scuff-scuff on the sidewalk.

He turned onto Maple Street and jogged past the high school. It was dark except for a single light on the ground floor, in the janitor's office. He stopped for a moment as he saw a lighted phone booth, dug into his pants for change, called her number. The telephone rang and rang but no one picked up. He hung up and ran on as the returned coins jingled down behind him.

After a little while he left the last streetlight behind, and the sidewalk as well. The stars, now that his eyes were adapting, gave enough light to distinguish the lighter tone of the asphalt from the dark of the shoulder. He stepped onto the pavement and ran on that since he could no longer see obstacles on the berm. His shins stabbed, but he didn't feel it.

The rising ground levelled and then began to fall away. He ran on. The cool breeze, still from behind him, brought the scents of pine woods and turned earth and of the dark. Occasionally as he ran the starlight allowed him to distinguish the remains of disused logging roads zigzagging off into black masses of woods.

Sometime later the moon began to rise behind him, throwing a little more light on the road ahead. He turned left then into one of the side roads, a paved one, a little broader than the others, which were unpaved. The trees overhead, their interlaced branches rustling and sighing sadly in the dark wind, cut off the stars until he could make out the road only by looking off to the side of it. He ran on.

The way curved gradually to the right and began to climb, easily at first, then steeper. little by little. Through an opening in the trees the moonlight fell on a little group of ponds. The wind from the dark places sent wavelets rippling across their surface, but their depths remained lightless and mysterious.

The grade steepened and bore to the left. A low chuckle of running water grew from ahead. The road emerged from the trees and seconds later the bridge echoed loudly as his feet pounded across its surface. The straight stretch followed and his breaths came faster, shorter, forcing more of the cool dark air into his lungs.

The straight ended and the road, shining now as the moon, rising, became brighter, curved right again and grew very steep.

A hundred short, powerful strokes of his legs and he was at the top. Then, after a short level at the crest, the pavement began its curve downward into the sleeping valley. Leaning back, he seemed to flow down the hill, expending the minimum of energy, letting gravity ease him smoothly downward into the valley.

Better take it easy on the downhill, said a voice in his memory. He looked ahead across the valley, over the lonely yellow lights of farmhouses, and made out the loom of the Hill beyond them, blotting out the stars for an impossible height above the earth.

Automatically a part of his mind flicked over the inputs from lungs, muscles, tendons, joints, heart; relax the shoulders, it ordered, bring the head up a little more, lengthen the stride. Left leg, holding up well, Calves, loose. Lower legs, increasingly painful, but that was to be expected. Jeans chafing at the crotch; minor. Air getting colder; breathe around the tongue, warming it for the lungs.

He was down in the valley now, pounding along on the right side of the two-lane. It was fairly bright now and he moved to the berm. The softness and slight unevenness helped his legs. Doing well. Shorten the stride again now that the ground's level.

The headlights of a pickup gleamed from farther down the valley, swept over the runner's head, settled on him as it drew closer. The old farmer driving saw a dark figure running slowly but gracefully, symmetrically, heels just brushing the ground at the end of each stride, swinging along with the totally relaxed and comfortable appearance of a loafing long-distance runner. One arm was doubled to the chest but the rhythm was still perfect.

The pickup clattered by and Phil was lost in darkness for a moment until his eyes readapted.

The wind freshened but it was still behind him. A dog barked somewhere off in the valley. Another, ahead, answered with a higher-pitched bark, almost a yelp. A light-colored blur came running out into the moonlit road. It kept pace with the runner for a few yards before, satisfied with his smell and his steady movements, trotted back into its own territory.

The road began to rise again some time after that and the crest of Porcupine Hill disappeared. The pavement narrowed again to one lane and he moved back off the shoulder to stay away from the shadowy ditches that paralleled them. His stride grew shorter, the steps closer together, the thrusts of his legs briefer but more demanding. He rounded the first switchback and the grade steepened. He rounded the second presently and, some hundreds of yards farther on, the last. His breath panted loudly, mixing with the sighing of the dark wind.

The road grew too steep to take straight on. He began to zig-zag across it, then was forced to plant his feet sidewise. The pace was agonizingly slow. With each step he had to lift his entire weight six more inches straight up.

The red lights blinked on in his head, lungs, and legs. He kept going, but slowed even more, each step seeming the prelude to a stop. The leg pains were gone, lost in the outcry from the rest of the body. They were numb, leaden. But they still moved.

Upward. Another two hundred yards, some remote part of his mind estimated.

Blood supply to the stomach had been cut off long before; it had contracted to a compact mass, squeezing the rich blood out to the muscles. Now his body began to economize on other, less vital oxygen demands. He blacked out for a moment but snapped back before his stride broke. It hurt. Everything hurt. The world was a mass of pain and he felt it all. The left leg refused a thrust and began to drag uselessly.

The grade suddenly ended and, clownlike, he stepped on his left foot with his right and went down in a tangle of arms and legs. His body was content to lie there, motionless, and refused to get up again. Red-hot shafts of air tore in and out of his throat.

Gradually the reddish haze cleared and he was able to roll off the roadway.

The earth was cold and he spread himself on it for its coldness against his fevered body. In a few minutes he was able to take back control of his lungs and suck deeper, slower breaths. Feeling, and with it pain, began to replace the numbness in his legs. One by one the red lights winked out, leaving a terrible weakness and trembling muscles.

Presently he tried to sit up.

Yes, he was at the top. There was the sign, dark against the starry sky, dotted now with moonlit clouds. There was the valley, spread below him, and the silvered clouds shining in the moonlight above it. He stared for long minutes, astonished at the world's beauty.

After a few more minutes he was able to stand. He leaned against the sign and tried his legs. The left was strained somehow, in the thigh or the crotch, but he could walk, though he limped pretty bad.

He took out her letter again and opened the envelope. It was crumpled now and damp. There was enough moonlight to read it by.

Dear Phil,

By the time you read this I will no longer be in town. I'm leaving and will not return.

I made a deal with the Board. I am resigning, effective immediately, and they are to reinstate you in school. My leaving town was part of the bargain too, but I would have anyway. Except for you, there is nothing to keep me here. And I can't have you.

Go back to school, Philip. Do whatever they want, but get your diploma; then leave. There's nothing here for you either. I know you will be a doctor someday, as you dream of being; and you will be a fine one, too.

I wish there were some way we could make it work, but I can't see any. You won't hear from me again, and please don't try to find me. You'll see me again, though. You'll see me in the eyes of every woman you ever meet throughout your life.

Remember me, my love. You are the bravest and noblest person I have ever known. I will always love you.

Cheshire.

He slowly wadded the little piece of paper up and stuffed it deep into his trouser pocket and sat still and looked out over the valley again. Here and there the moonlight silvered the sheetmetal roof of a farmhouse, here and there a yellow light glimmered distantly in the dark valley, under the rushing clouds.

She's right, he thought, hugging his legs to him against the chill that was beginning to invade his body now that the warmth of the run was ebbing. *Cheshire's right. She sees things very clearly.*

And my mom's right, too; and, each in his own way, so was Joe Brentano, lying at that moment sleepless and motionless in an expensive private room; and so were Heckathorne and Ashberne, and the rest of the board members and angry parents, worried for their children, that they should grow up honestly and with as little pain as possible; and even Alex Ryan, even she was right, for she needed and so she took. And each of them acted out of love, love for him, love for a girl, love of children, love of self. Each acted out of love.

And each was right.

All that's left, he thought, *is for me to make my own decisions. Not to turn to others, not to obey them, or be guided blindly by their well-meaning advice. My own choice.*

He studied the bare ground under him. It too was glowing and ethereal in the openhanded moonlight. *The Hill,* he thought. *I didn't 'conquer' it. No one ever had.* It made him stronger, little by little, until he was at last able to climb it.

164

If there were no difficulties in life, no trials, no obstacles, there could be no success or possibility of achievement.

He stretched his strained leg out along the unearthly ground and doubled it back to his hip, forcing the knee repeatedly to the ground to stretch the thigh and groin. It hurt like hell but after a few reps the strained muscles relaxed and felt a little better.

There was a Hill to climb, he thought, *when I was in a wheelchair, and when I was on crutches, but I finally walked.* Staying in Raymondsville was another hill to climb. And to be able to help other people, to be a doctor, that was still another; a long way off, a very high one, but visible ahead in the distance.

He got up and turned away from the sign at the crest, and from the moon, and from the valley; set his face toward the dark downward slope toward home. It would be a long walk back, and his legs were in terrible shape. He'd take a couple of days off and give them time to recover.

Damned if I know how you do it, he thought, *but there's always another hill visible from the crest of the last one. And for that, we thank you from the bottom of our hearts.*

He'd have to start keeping times on these Hill workouts. He'd really run at a dreadfully slow pace tonight.

Well, that would improve.

THE END

THE HEMLOCK COUNTY NOVELS

This was my first novel, and no one has ever read it until now, though I adapted a few passages for a later book. For any awkwardness, my apologies!

If you enjoyed this novel, you'll find my writing improved (I hope) in the later Hemlock County novels, *The Dead of Winter, Winter in the Heart, As The Wolf Loves Winter,* and *Thunder on the Mountain.* Originally published by Forge/Macmillan, they're currently available from Northampton House Press in print and ebook.

Northampton House Press

Established in 2011, Northampton House Press publishes selected fiction, nonfiction, memoir, and poetry. Check out our list at www.northampton-house.com, and Like us on Facebook – "Northampton House Press" – as we showcase more innovative works from brilliant new talents.

Printed in the USA
CPSIA information can be obtained
at www.ICGtesting.com
LVHW091805300624
784350LV00005B/609

9 781950 668267